Though the Bodies Fall

Though the Bodies Fall

Noel O'Regan

GRANTA

Granta Publications, 12 Addison Avenue, London, W11 4QR

First published in Great Britain by Granta Books, 2023

A CIP catalogue record for this book
is available from the British Library.

1   3   5   7   9   10   8   6   4   2

ISBN 978 1 78378 948 1
eISBN 978 1 78378 949 8

Typeset in Garamond by Patty Rennie
Printed and bound by CPI Group (UK) Ltd, Croydon, CR0 4YY

www.granta.com

For my parents, Denis & Elizabeth

'Looking down from great heights brings the urge to fall and end the terror of falling.'

John McGahern, *Amongst Women*

'Piece of shit. Stupid piece of shit. You're a real stupid piece of shit.'

BoJack Horseman, *BoJack Horseman*

This was, what, almost thirty years ago now? But he still has a clear sight of it. The weary cycle out the headland after training, hurley and helmet balanced on the handlebar. Sea and sky a steely mirror of one another. Home finally up ahead: pebble-dashed bungalow, wildflower-burst field rising to the cliffs.

There. Up by the cliffs. His mother and another figure. A visitor.

The sense of something lurching inside him, like during a sudden, precipitous drop. Near falling off the bike by the house. Dash through the field, flattening flowers he had no interest to name then but can now: white campion, cowslip, long-stalked crane's bill, speedwell.

As he neared, he slowed his pace, not wanting to spook the visitor. The man was in his seventies at least, maybe eighties. He wore a navy tweed suit and newly polished black loafers. The shine off them was such that he must have been scrubbing for hours. He also wore a matching hat with a groove running along the top of it. It was called a homburg, his mother later told him. 'I'm sorry,' the man said to his mother – he hadn't seemed to notice Micheál's presence yet; perhaps his eyesight wasn't the best – 'but I really must go.' The way he said it, as if he was late for a train or an appointment. 'I can't keep her waiting any longer.'

And with that he was gone.

PART ONE

1

The visitor leaves in the early dawn. Micheál Burns stands at the bedroom window, careful not to touch the white, flower-patterned net curtain, as he watches the figure – a thirty-something bachelor farmer named James Walsh – hesitate in the front yard. You could almost believe that he's stopping to take in the view: the choppy bay, the frail branch of dune and rock that is the Maharees to the south-west, the purple mountains across the water, swollen with the threat of further rain. After a moment, Walsh turns left, in the direction of the front gate, the road back in along the headland and his home outside Ardfert, about eight miles away. He had staggered all the way here last night in a downpour; now he will walk all the way back.

Once he has gone out of sight, Micheál searches the bedroom for clean clothes. The hangers in the wardrobe are bare, except for one from which a burgundy tie dangles. Beside the unmade bed are a heap of his clothes, all long since in need of washing. He had been hoping to get a few more wears out of what he'd on him last night, his black jeans and red woollen jumper, but they are now dumped, sopping, beside the nightstand. The runners he'd been wearing were discarded in the hall; they'd need a day at least under a rad to dry out. In the end, he picks a pair of food-stained blue jeans and a grey T-shirt from the heap. He gives both armpits of the T-shirt a sniff. It'd do.

In the kitchen, he fills the kettle. His bare feet on the cold tiles wake him up a bit more. He takes a bowl from the sink and washes it under the tap water, picking at a stubborn piece of porridge with his thumbnail until it falls away. Out the window, he sees seagulls hovering in the air, suspended. As he waits for the kettle to boil, his gaze is drawn to the picture of Christ hanging above the fireplace, a flickering red light where his heart should be. He keeps meaning to change the bulb, or take it out entirely.

Once the tea is made, he sips it, even knowing that it's too hot. He still has some of the bone-deep cold in him from last night. He considers taking a hit of whiskey, but it probably is too early for that sort of thing.

In the sitting room, Sammy appears out from the spot between the TV and east-facing window where his bed is nestled: a strange position, but one he likes. There used to be a thin, plastered wall separating the kitchen from the sitting room at the inland-end of the house, but his parents had knocked that down when he was young. He realises now that its absence allowed for a better view from the kitchen, even the hallway, of the country road, the wrought-iron gate and rise up to the house. The Border collie ambles between the tan-coloured couch and wicker armchair into the kitchen, looks at the cup half-filled with oats on the counter, the carton of milk next to the saucepan. Then he stares at his empty bowl beside the rad.

'Alright, alright,' Micheál says. He opens the press under the sink, takes out a near-empty bag of dog food. Only then does Sammy's tail wag. Micheál pours so much that the food overflows from the bowl. He pats the dog's flank as Sammy digs in. He'd been brilliant last night. The security light in the yard hadn't come on when Walsh arrived; he must have given the front of the house too wide a berth. Instead it was Sammy who'd sensed him, barking incessantly by the front door. It was just in time, too; Walsh had been most of the way up the field by the time Micheál reached him.

After breakfast, he looks at the plastic-framed clock hanging above the doorway leading into the hall, its glass cover long since lost. Half seven. If he left now, he'd be into the village before the school rush. He did need to pick up a few things at Brenda's: a carton of milk, pan of bread, more dog food for Sammy, soap, toilet paper, those detergent capsules that look like tortellini. The heap had to be tackled at some point; it might as well be today.

He puts on his boots and jacket and goes outside, Sammy racing ahead, wet nose to wet earth. A blast of wind rushes in off the bay, knocking Micheál off balance for a moment till he plants one foot a step behind him. He looks at the field of long grass and wildflowers beside the house, the way it rises like a wave until, near the cliff edge, changing to stone, mud and sea thrift. The highest cliffs south of Moher, his mother had always told him. The end of the headland is a good mile in length, but it is only here, on their land, that it rises so starkly.

Rain is falling further out the bay, obscuring most of the Seven Hogs, though the nearest of the cluster of islands,

Illauntannig, is still visible. Judging by the direction of the wind, the squall will likely race him the four miles or so into the village. It's fifty-fifty whether he'll arrive dry or drowned.

II

Micheál's grandparents bought the bungalow and surrounding land from its previous owners, the Lynches, in 1971. His grandfather had been in the Guards, a sergeant in the Tralee barracks; his grandmother had been a primary-school teacher in Balloonagh Girls' National School. Both were recently retired, their four children all grown, so this house was something of a retirement treat to themselves. They had always liked bringing the children out to Ballyheigue in the summers in their temperamental Morris Minor. Micheál has tried to imagine their excitement when they first moved, the view from the bungalow 'postcard-ready', as his grandmother said. Their nearest neighbours were not very close when compared to the semi-detached house in Oakpark Terrace in Tralee, but they were, if not friendly, at least welcoming. His grandmother found the sea air particularly invigorating.

It happened for the first time about three months after they moved in, according to his mother, who heard about it when she called out the next day. Their first visitor was a young man with the drink on him. She wouldn't have noticed the man at all, Micheál's grandmother said, but that he passed the bungalow within the glow of light reaching out the kitchen window when she happened to be at the sink, washing the ware after tea.

'Tom,' she said. 'Tom.'

'What?' Micheál's grandfather said, startling awake from his position in the armchair by the fireplace.

'There's someone outside.'

It was a cloudless night with a near-full moon, so they spotted him with ease, walking through the field, rising with the land, even as it rose towards its end. His grandfather shouted after the man, who was staggering and appeared to be ranting to himself. The name 'Mary' or it might have been 'Marie' came back on the wind. His grandmother pulled her cardigan tight around her as his grandfather made to march towards the cliffs, but as he set off, they saw the man reach high enough that he seemed to graze the stars, and then he disappeared.

'Oh God,' his grandmother exclaimed.

His grandfather drove to the Garda station in the village that night and informed the sergeant, whom he knew from his years in the Guards. 'He must have lost his bearings with the load of drink in him,' the sergeant said, and his grandfather agreed. 'He seemed oiled, alright.' Micheál imagines the sergeant poking at the fire in the barracks, keeping his eyes on it as he speaks again: 'That happens a bit now and again up there, Tom. People losing their way, falling. I'm surprised Lynch didn't say something to you about that, now – it was bad form by him. But it's just something to keep an eye on. Nothing a fence or a sign won't stop, I'm sure.'

His grandfather and Uncle Mikey put up the fence the following weekend, Mikey cycling out from Tralee to help.

They trailed it all along the cliff edge. He also put a wooden post up by the front gate, a sign on it warning in clear block lettering:

PRIVATE PROPERTY

DANGEROUS CLIFF AHEAD

NO TRESPASSERS

Neither the sign nor the fence worked, of course. Near Christmas of that first year, it happened again. In the open show of daylight this time. He was at the fence before they noticed him. Micheál's grandfather ran towards him, even with his bad hip, but the man had gone over long before his grandfather reached the fence.

After that, they realised that there wasn't much that could be done. There was talk for a while about getting guard dogs, but his grandmother had been bitten by a neighbour's Jack Russell when a child and had a wild fear of dogs. 'Anything with teeth that sharp shouldn't be trusted,' she said.

The fence is gone now, as is the sign. Micheál is unsure how many more visits happened during his grandparents' time. According to his mother, they never spoke about it. His grandmother did talk for a while about selling or moving, but his grandfather refused to leave, saying they wouldn't let those hell-bound cowards drive them out of their dream home.

3

Micheál bursts into Brenda's Newsagents, holding the door open behind him. Brenda looks up from the newspaper she has splayed on the counter beside the till, grins. 'A wild one, is it?'

Micheál grunts. 'Is it alright if Sammy comes in? I can't leave him out in that.'

'Go on, so,' she says. 'Just make sure he buys something while he's here.'

Another grunt from Micheál as he lowers his sodden hood. Sammy comes inside and gives himself a little shake. When he trots up to the counter, Brenda kneels beside him and scratches behind his ear, the spot he loves. Micheál walks along the narrow aisle towards them. The shop has changed little since his own childhood days: the island of shelving in the centre, the encircling aisle where two people would struggle to stand side by side, the esoteric arrangement of goods: plastic buckets and spades stacked beside firelighters and tinned tuna. You wouldn't see many shops like this anymore; it's a testament to Brenda's mother's legacy, and Brenda's own fortitude, that the shop remains open, particularly with a Costcutter and Centra also on Main Street.

'Haven't seen you in a while,' Brenda says, standing. 'Everything alright out on Land's End?'

'Ah, you know.'

'How's Áine?'

'Sure you're more likely than me to know how she's doing. It should be me asking you, really.'

Brenda and Áine had been best friends growing up and

still keep in touch. Sometimes, he suspects that his sister had told Brenda more than she should have. He often saw Áine's worry mirrored in her, mostly in her attempts to get him away from the bungalow: to train the Under-14s camogie team, to join the Tidy Towns committee, to try out the local Men's Shed – though he'd have been at least twenty years younger than all the other members. Once she invited him to take part in the local book club she'd organised. He'd gone as far as to read the one they had coming up – *Barkskins* by Annie Proulx – but, on the day, he felt unable to leave.

A teenager in a grey and maroon uniform rushes into the shop. Her school shoes squeak on the floor as she grabs a bottle of water from the fridge, plucks strawberry-flavoured chewing gum from the stand by the till, and places both items on the counter.

'Need fresh breath for someone, eh, Laura?' Brenda asks, scanning the gum.

The girl blushes.

'Don't worry, I won't tell your mother.'

As the girl leaves, she shouts back, 'Thanks, Junior.'

'Nice girl,' Brenda says. 'Quality camogie player, too.'

Micheál nods as he gathers his few items. He wonders how she feels about being called 'Junior' by someone so much younger. It's a nickname she's had since childhood, though he can never bring himself to use it. The name is a legacy of her mother. Brenda Senior. She had a reputation as the village's resident activist. Mostly this involved going around to the nearby houses, asking people to sign petitions, to give money for this or that cause. She used to have different pamphlets and manifestos available in the shop, including Republican materials. Her family had a history in insurrection, apparently. One of Micheál's earliest memories is of Brenda Senior having a heated argument with Fr Burke on Main Street; this would have been during the divorce referendum – back in the mid-nineties, mind, when the Church still had some bit of hold on the place. 'Do you know how some people have a delicate stomach for certain foods,' Micheál's mother said to him at one point. 'Well, Brenda's like that. Only it's with injustice, as she sees it; she can't stomach it.' As for the 'Junior', men were always doing it, after all – 'Frank Junior, Mike Senior, John-Joe III; they never get enough of it!' – so why couldn't she? Brenda Junior hadn't much say in it.

Micheál pays for his few things, glances outside, where the rain continues to dart down the street.

'Do you fancy a cuppa?' Brenda asks.

'Go on, so,' he says.

After a few minutes, she brings two mugs out from the back, hands the Kit Kat mug to him. Good portion of milk, no sugar – the usual. 'That'll be three euro,' she says. He freezes with the cup halfway to his mouth. Brenda laughs at his expression. 'I'm only messing, you gom. Drink it.'

IV

Micheál's grandfather died just before Micheál was born, about ten years after his grandparents moved out to the headland. His mother said it was as a result of an illness, though she never specified the kind. All she said was that he refused to go to the doctor and by the end his skin was a pale yellow, not too different from the colour of the strand below Ballyheigue village. 'It was as if the land around was reclaiming him,' she said. His grandmother managed a few years out on the headland by herself, but then she sprained her wrist in a fall as she walked down to collect the post, and when she broke a hip a month later, it became clear that she was too frail to live alone.

Micheál never knew why his parents moved to the headland. After all, it would have made more sense for his grandmother to move in with them in town. Looking back, he also struggles to understand why it had to be them – what about Uncle Dinny, Mikey or Aunt Sheila? Dinny didn't even have a family and only worked odd jobs; it'd have been much easier for him to move. But, for whatever reason, his mother insisted: his grandmother could not leave the headland, and it had to be them who moved. One of his biggest regrets – and he has many – is that he never asked why.

Micheál was six at the time and felt like his world was crumbling. He had to leave the estate where all his best friends lived, had to stop playing football with the Austin Stacks Under-8s, even though they gave out free Taytos and Coke after every training session. 'They have a team in Ballyheigue,' his mother promised, though she didn't tell him that it was a hurling team, not football. When he found out, he bawled: 'I don't want to be a hurler!' A compromise of sorts allowed him to stay in his school in Tralee. Since his father taught in Balloonagh Girls' National School, a five-minute walk from his all-boys school, Holy Family, he could drop Micheál off in the mornings. Áine would start in the local primary school on Kerry Head the following September, where his mother was also due to begin work part-time in the office, having given up teaching after becoming pregnant with Micheál. Saoirse would also go to school there, when the time came.

After the move, he soon noticed how his family stood out in the area. Most of the land far out the headland was farm-land, with one or two B&Bs nearby. Their place was neither. The nearest neighbours, the Spillanes, who owned the land across the road, and the Dwyers, who owned the land bordering the sea to the north, were all cordial, offering greetings and polite enquiries when meeting in the village or on the road, but Micheál sensed an unspoken divide.

Still, after a while, he began to settle. Uncertain, he went to a few of the hurling training sessions and found that he liked it: the ash hurls clashing, the frantic chase around the pitch and hurried smack of the sliotar, the shock reverberating up his arm with each strike. He made friends with a couple of his teammates, Tuan Dowling and Stephen Murphy. Tuan, all red hair and wiriness, lived in the village, while Stephen's family lived near the primary school in Glenderry, about halfway out the headland. Stephen and most of his siblings had the jet-black hair and dark complexion that some said signified 'Spanish blood'. The bainisteoir called him 'Iglesias', though the nickname failed to catch on.

The three of them soon spent most evenings and weekends together, adventuring around the headland: scaling the rocks along the coast outside the village, sometimes swimming at Meenogahane Pier and daring each other out towards the stack in the harbour known as the 'Horricles', sneaking through farmers' land to summit Triskmore and search out An Claí Rua, the Red Ditch, where ghosts were said to dwell. It was Stephen and Tuan who first brought Micheál to the stone fort about half a mile to the north of his house. The ruins were, technically, on Dwyer's land, but there was a right of way in place. It became a hideout, where they imagined themselves as watchmen keeping an eye out for Viking ships or the Luftwaffe, smugglers, or pirates coming ashore to plunder.

After these forays across the headland, Micheál would arrive home exhausted. Once dinner was ready, he was forced to bring his grandmother her food in bed. She was in the single room next to the bathroom, having given the room with the double bed to Micheál's parents. He hated bringing her food, disliked spending any time around her, really – particularly in her room. She had that stale, old-person smell, her bones were too visible, running up her arms and protruding from her neck, and then there was the chatter of her false teeth with every bite of the food. The smell, though coming from her, seemed to have radiated out to every crevice of the room. All these things worked their way under his skin, made him squirm. Micheál was ten when she died, and though he felt bad for having those thoughts, for a long time afterwards he could still hear the chatter and chomp of those false teeth, still caught that smell whenever he passed her room.

5

Micheál says goodbye to Brenda, plastic bag of shopping in hand. His bike, a rusty twelve-speed Raleigh, is a wounded creature splayed against the shop wall. He forces the bulging shopping bag on to the rack behind the frayed saddle, the luggage bar snapping down, squashing. He hops on the bike and pedals off, Sammy trotting after him.

The village is quiet at this time, now that the school rush has passed. Cycling across the square, he glances left at the long stretch of strand, stony near the dunes and sky-pooled towards the sea. Sandpipers skitter along the shoreline, something manic in their movements, rushing seaward in search of food, fleeing before the next wave arrives. The turreted stone entrance to Ballyheigue Castle looms to his right, leading up to the part-restored castle and surrounding nine-hole golf course. He has never played the course, though he did sneak on to it once, on a summer's day when he was seven or eight, with Tuan and Stephen. They went to a water trap by one of the greens out of sight of the clubhouse and fished golf balls from the stout-coloured water, Stephen having had the idea to fill a plastic bag with the recovered balls and sell them for fifty pence each down on the strand. They'd practically lived on ice-cream for a week afterwards with the spoils.

Micheál feels the familiar tension rise in him as he cycles out past the holiday homes on the outskirts of the village – white, flimsy things with a hollow sense to them now in the off season. He has been away longer than planned, the tea and conversation with Brenda stretching. Though it's unlikely that another visitor would call so soon on the heels of another

17

– and early morning, post-dawn, has never been a common time for such a visit – he knows well by now that this feeling will not settle until he is home.

He pedals a little harder, though not enough to trouble Sammy, who patters, tongue out, beside him. Blackberries decorate the hedges along the road, most already withering amid bell-shaped fuchsia. He passes the primary school at Glenderry, bunting flapping from the eaves, the orange and black colours of the local club, who have a county championship final against Abbeydorney at the weekend. Through one of the windows, he sees hands raised, a screen flickering.

As he cycles further out the headland, spined first by Maulin Mountain, then Triskbeg and finally the cone-shaped Triskmore, the holiday homes and B&Bs lessen, and farmland grows more prominent: the old stone walls, the hoofed-on ground by the feeding troughs, the Friesians in the fields all standing apart, staking out their own piece of earth. At one point, Sammy barks and a trio of starlings burst out of the roadside hedge. Near the end of the headland, the southern flank steepens sharply; from the road it looks like the stone-fenced fields slide straight down into the sea, as if the headland is trying to shed all that clings to its skin.

At land's end, the bungalow comes into view, perched on a brief plateau halfway up the cliff, just prior to its final steep ascent. South-facing, over the bay, the white pebble-dashed exterior like some tourist's dream of a rural Irish cottage. During the summer months, particularly since the headland has become part of the 'Wild Atlantic Way', he's often seen people park their cars to take pictures, the clichéd mix of rustic bungalow and rugged vista too much to pass without capturing.

The front gate is closed, which is a good sign. A visitor is usually beyond the point of shutting a gate after themselves. He rests the bike against the side of the house and walks up towards the field, the cliff. No obvious trails through the high grass, nor of any movement up by the cliff, apart from a pair of gannets floating in and out of view. That gnawing feeling eased for now, he walks back towards the house.

Inside, he puts the shopping on the table and pours water into Sammy's bowl. The sound of his rushed lapping fills the kitchen. As he stands by the sink, a heavy tiredness on him – he must have only had an hour or two of fitful sleep last night – Micheál sees the cargo ship outside the window, not far off Brandon Point. Energised, he goes to his laptop on the kitchen table and clicks on the Marine Watch website. His notebook is up on the counter beside the sink, the Roman numerals XXXIII written in red ink on the cover. He copies the online information in his neatest handwriting.

5 October
9.57 a.m.
Victoria T
Bulk carrier
Flag: PA
Port: CAS, MA
13.1/11.0 knots

High tide isn't for another couple of hours yet. It'd likely stall out by Illauntannig and wait for the right time before making its way to port in Fenit.

Underneath the ship entry, he adds:

Starlings (x3)
Sandpipers (x5/6)
Ring-billed gull
Gannet (x2)

Afterwards, Micheál fills the kettle and sets it to boil. As he waits, he feels a sudden stirring in him and walks down the hallway and into the bathroom. He stands over the opened toilet and unzips. He takes his self in his hand and feels a sudden embarrassment, as if he's being watched. He shakes his head. People need to shit and piss; this is no different. It is done quickly enough, and he flushes and washes his hands in the sink. Dammit. Soap. He forgot to buy soap.

His mobile phone rings in the kitchen. Hands half-dried, he rushes down the hallway, picks the phone up with a still-damp hand. Áine. Of course it's Áine. Who else could it be? With a deep breath, he hits the answer button, puts the phone to his ear. For a moment, that earlier sense of embarrassment returns, as if she knows what he'd been doing. Or maybe it is just the jab of guilt he always feels when about to speak to Áine – or Saoirse, for that matter; though it's been a long while since they last spoke.

'Áine, you're well?'

'I am, Mick.'

'And the family?'

'They're grand, although Ryan has the chickenpox, so he's being a particular joy.'

'I can imagine,' Micheál says, struggling to stifle a yawn.

Áine's tone shifts. Concern creeps in. 'A late one, was it?'

'It was, alright.'

Silence at the other end of the line.

'How's Sammy?' she asks, changing the subject.

'Good, good. Eating me out of house and home, you know the way.'

'Look, Mick, I'm going to be coming down on Saturday.'

'Oh yeah?'

'Yeah, I promised Brenda I'd pay her a visit this weekend, and I was hoping I'd have a few words with yourself, too, while I'm down. There's something I'd like to discuss.'

Micheál frowns. Strange that Brenda said nothing about the visit this morning. It seemed like she hadn't heard from Áine in a few weeks. 'Oh, right,' he says. 'I can set up your room for you, so, if you'd like?'

'No, no, that's alright, Mick. I'm just down for the day.'

'Right,' he says.

'I was hoping to call out to you in the afternoon, after I see Brenda. If that's alright?'

'Of course, Áine, sure it's your house as much as it is mine.'

He catches the slightest hesitation before she says, 'Yeah, right, so I'll see you on Saturday so?'

'I'm looking forward to it,' he says.

VI

The first time he saw one of them, it was during his seventh summer – one of those rare, baking weeks when the bay looks almost tropical. He was playing with his hurley out the back of the house, striking the sliotar off the wall, when a man sprinted past, as if something was chasing him. Micheál watched him run until the point where the field steepened, when the man tripped and fell, near-swallowed by the long grass. Micheál ran into the house. 'What are you doing?' his mother asked as he dragged a chair from the table to the sink, climbed on it and filled a glass with water from the tap. 'The man fell down. He's thirsty.'

His mother ordered him down from the chair, told him to stay inside while she went to help the man. He wandered down to his bedroom, played with his toy cars, his Teenage Mutant Ninja Turtles. When he returned to the kitchen he noticed the glass, still on the counter by the sink. She'd forgotten it. He thought to bring it out, to help, but remained inside. As she'd asked. She came back some time later, with a look on her face that Micheál found difficult to read. Something was torn in her, he thought.

When he was a little older, his mother sat him down at the kitchen table and explained that the thirsty man that day had been a 'visitor', and these were sad people who sometimes came here needing help. He hadn't seen a visitor before that day, or since, because they often arrived at night or before Micheál and his sisters woke, the visitors eager to 'find help' with the rising sun at their backs.

Now that Micheál knew about them, he was put in charge of keeping his sisters from making the same discovery. On the rare occasions when visitors arrived in the evenings, while they were still awake, Micheál's mother gave him a clear set of instructions: feed his sisters (if they hadn't eaten already) by microwaving one of the ready meals in the fridge; don't let them go outside until the visitor has left; if his parents had not returned by seven o'clock, he was to make sure they got ready for bed. Lights were to be out by eight o'clock for Saoirse, half eight for Áine. He was allowed stay up till nine o'clock, but was expected to go to bed then, whether or not his parents had returned. Sometimes, despite the instructions, he would sneak outside and watch them. On a couple of occasions, he caught Áine trying to sneak out, too, and, with difficulty, dragged her inside.

One evening – he was ten, maybe eleven – he snuck out only to find both sisters, having climbed out one of their bedroom windows, staring up towards the cliffs. It must have been sometime in spring, as he remembers the coconut scent of gorse heavy in the twilight air, a red gash over the mountains on the far side of the bay, near Gleann na nGealt, where the sun set that time of year. The light had faded enough that his parents were two standing-stone silhouettes, either side of another doubled-over shape, swaying back and forth.

Saoirse tugged at Áine's dressing gown, pointed to the shadows. 'But I want him to read me the story.'

'He's busy,' Áine said. And Micheál realised that she knew. He had failed to keep it from her.

'But he said he would!' Saoirse shouted, loud enough that the distant figures stirred. After a few moments, one of the standing stones moved towards them.

'Get in,' Micheál hissed, trying to force them back to the house, but Saoirse screamed again and Áine threw him a look that seemed to say this was his fault, somehow, though she was the one who had brought her outside. As the shadow neared, he tried desperately to shoo them inside, and took a hold of Saoirse's hand, but this only set her to screaming again.

The shadow grew and grew and then became his father. 'What's going on here?' he asked, a spike of frustration in the words.

Saoirse jumped, startled, having not seen him approach. She began to sob. 'It's okay, my little lurcher,' he said, rubbing her head, his nickname for her capturing her slight form and general skittishness. 'Come on, everyone inside.' Micheál frowned at the readiness with which his sisters followed his father's orders when they had so casually dismissed his own. 'Yeah, get inside,' he added. Áine raised her eyes to the feathered clouds, a fading contrail.

His father herded them into the kitchen, hovered at the threshold. A loud sound, almost like a howl, from outside. His sisters stiffened, clenched hands. Micheál imagined a wolf attacking Spillane's cows, teeth sinking into hide. His father's long dark curls seemed to dance in the wind as he looked towards the cliffs. 'Right, off to bed with you.'

'But my story,' Saoirse pleaded.

'I can't tonight, pet. Your brother is going to read to you instead, okay?'

'Fine,' she said, sniffling, her obvious disappointment stinging Micheál. Normally, she liked it when he read to her, would sometimes search him out, picture book in hand. She laughed at the voices he did, the sound effects.

'You'll do this for me, champ?' his father asked.

'Fine,' Micheál said, trying his best to match Saoirse's tone. Let her know he wanted this as little as she did.

'Good lad.'

And this next moment remains the clearest image Micheál has in his mind of his father: standing at the threshold of the house in his muddied boots and heather-coloured coat, which hid his own lurcher frame that had never quite filled out. The red gash in the sky near extinguished behind him. He stood there a moment longer, smiling, as if to take them in, and with that he turned and was soon a shadow again, returning to the visitor.

Micheál thought little unusual about the visitors, at first. But then he began to notice the odd glance his mother and father sometimes received when they travelled into the village for groceries or when dropping him off to hurling training, and realised that the polite but definite distance between them and the neighbours had little to do with their not running a B&B or a farm.

One day, he, Stephen and Tuan went hunting ghosts near An Claí Rua, imaginary proton packs at hand. By then, they had begun to stay overnight at each other's houses – Tuan's twice and once at Stephen's – and so Micheál invited them to come to his that night.

Stephen picked up a sharp flint of stone, stared across heather, bog. He flung it far, skimming it through the air, and they watched it fall, land without sound, sinking into wet, grabbing earth. Moments earlier, this would have spooked ghosts into flight, and they would have fired, careful not to cross plasma streams. Now, though, the ghosts had stilled, the game finished.

'We're not allowed stay over,' Stephen said, still looking towards where the stone had landed.

'Why?'

Tuan shrugged; Stephen eyed the ground, as if for more stones.

Micheál felt his face flush. The friendship had contained this unspoken fault line, and though it remained unsaid, he sensed that all of them could feel it now, out in the open, exposed. Looking back, Brenda was the only friend of any of them who stayed over, and he knows that was due to Brenda Senior's want for defying the 'conservative status quo', as she'd have put it.

His parents were clearly unbothered by each side-eyed glance or rumour, so Micheál decided to be too. His parents were a team, was how he thought of them. Around the house, if one was preparing the dinner, the other was helping them with their homework; if one was hoovering, the other was hanging up the clothes or watering the potted geraniums on the front windowsills. Even in rest, they settled beside each other, watching TV, listening to the radio. They had a habit of buying two copies of a book, so they could read it at the same time, discuss its flaws and merits, share thoughts. And if at times it felt to Micheál like he and his sisters were on the outside of their team – or on the subs bench, anyway – he hoped that helping them while they helped the visitors would one day earn him a place on the inside.

7

A sound wakes him to darkness and the heavy weight of blankets. He stays as still as he can, listening. Had there been an actual sound, or was it just the clattering end to a dream? The security light isn't on. No noise from Sammy.

Micheál keeps his breathing shallow as he tries to listen more intently. There. A shrill gust. Maybe something was knocked over by the wind? The flowerpots on the windowsill, the rubbish. Or the recycling bin. Or maybe there had been no sound at all? He could have just woken himself up. The security light is off; Sammy's asleep. It was likely nothing. He closes his eyes and focuses on his breathing. In, out. In, out. He can feel the tug of sleep; it's still in range, despite the sound/not-sound. In, out. In, out.

Fuck it.

His runners are still under the rad. The outsides of them are dry now, but as soon as he slips his left foot in he feels the squelchy embrace of the insole. The right one is even worse. His coat is perched on the back of one of the kitchen chairs, the flashlight stationed at its spot on the counter by the door.

The security light clicks on as soon as he steps outside. A gust slaps flecks of water against his face, and he knows from the taste that it's of the sea rather than the sky. Everything is normal within the hemisphere of the light: the flowerpots rest on the sill, the bins stand upright. He glances down towards the road. The gate is closed, no vehicles are parked in view. When he turns towards the cliff the section of the field illuminated by the light is empty.

It was nothing. He should go back inside. Still, he walks towards the field. Once outside the touch of the security light, he lifts the flashlight and moves the beam in a slow, methodical manner from side to side as he climbs towards the cliffs. It takes him little time to confirm that the field is empty. Among the long grass and wildflowers, he watches amber lights flicker along the Maharees spit. At night, looking from this vantage point, you'd never think they were on dry land.

VIII

It happened, without warning, at work one day. His father was standing in front of his class, in the middle of a Geography lesson, when he hunched over and fell forward, hitting his temple off the corner of one of the wooden desks in the front row. They were later told that the blow to the head hadn't made a difference; the strength of the attack by his heart on the rest of him meant that he would have died anyway. Familial hypertrophic cardiomyopathy was the cause, a genetic disease that thickens heart muscle. Ever since, Micheál's mother demanded that he and his sisters get annual check-ups, to ensure they don't suffer their father's sudden fate. When the principal, Mr O'Donoghue, described how their father had died, he told them he'd been teaching the class about tectonic plates when it happened. Micheál has often wondered why he provided them with this detail.

His mother sank into a state of stunned withdrawal. She remained apart from Micheál and the girls, taking to her bed, or going for long walks around the headland. Always he watched her leave, afraid she would turn right once out the door. In her place, Micheál tried to be strong for his sisters. He only cried when he was alone. He took to watering the potted geraniums on the windowsill, which had been one of his father's favourite chores. He even started helping Saoirse with her homework. One evening, he left her with her head down at the kitchen table, shoulders curled in near her ears as she lined up her crayons beside her colouring book, set them neatly in order. The open page before her a fresh gale of colour. Áine sat at the far end of the table, her breathing ragged, head bowed. Was she crying? He started towards her, was about to ask if she was okay, when she glared up at him. 'Stop trying to be him,' Áine said. 'You're not him.' She rose from the table and retreated to her bedroom, schoolbooks held tight to her chest.

After a time, his mother returned to them, paler and skinnier than before, hair wilder. One night, when the girls had gone to bed, she sat across from him at the kitchen table and explained how things would be. Micheál was twelve, she said, old enough to help out with the visitors, now that his father no longer could. He stared at his mother's round, high-cheekboned face, the shape of which both he and Áine had inherited, along with her stockiness.

At the mention of her late husband, his mother glanced over Micheál's head at the blood-lit portrait of Christ on the wall and blessed herself. 'He would want you to help me with this,' she added.

'Jesus?' Micheál asked.

'Your father,' she said. 'It's simple. Just listen to these people, let them know that you are here for them. And never, ever judge them. They are in a dark, dark place, and we must try our best to bring them back into the light. Do you understand?'

Micheál nodded, hoping he looked as solemn as he felt.

'Good. It is tough work, Micheál, but it is God's work. And it is up to us to see that it is done, and that we save as many souls as we can.'

He nodded again.

9

The morning before Áine's visit, he looks around the house with his sister's eyes, and what he sees forces him on to his bike, a stiff south-westerly nudging him into the village. Supplies include a six-pack of yellow sponges, Dettol surface wipes, refuse bags, soap pads, bleach, Toilet Duck cleaning gel, Febreze fabric spray and some all-surface cloths. 'Don't tell Áine about any of this,' he says to Brenda as he leaves the shop.

'Right, so,' she says. He sees in her the struggle not to smile.

Back at the house, he plonks the bags down on the table and surveys the kitchen, wondering where to begin. The dirty plates and cups and cutlery are stacked in and around the sink; the counters are covered in a patchwork of stains of various colours and shapes, months' worth of overlapping cup marks like a knotted chain by the microwave, a debris field of crumbs by the toaster. The floor isn't much better, the tiles covered in boot prints and dog hair. Everywhere, the smell of wet mutt. And this is just the kitchen.

As he starts on the counters, he thinks again about Áine's coming here. What can she want to talk about? How important must it be that she is willing to come out the headland to see him? She hasn't stepped foot in the house since their mother's passing, well over a decade ago now. When they meet, it is in Ballyheigue, for a carvery with her family, or just for a cup of tea and a chat on the days that she comes down by herself, the first Sunday of every month. Like clockwork, or an obligation.

He scrubs furiously at the counter by the stove, but some of the stains refuse to disappear. They seem part of the surface now, seared on. No matter how much he scrubs and washes and bleaches, anyway, Áine is likely to notice things that he has missed or done wrong; that has always been her way.

X

It was four months after his father's death before a visitor arrived. Micheál was doing his homework in his bedroom when his mother called him from the kitchen. 'Micheál, get your shoes on quick. Hurry now.' When he reached the kitchen, shoes on but untied, she was set in his father's thick cream fleece, with the old brick of a flashlight in her hand, though a fair bit of light remained in the sky. 'Always be ready for a long stay out,' she'd tell him afterwards. 'These visits can last hours, sometimes.'

Micheál felt excited at the prospect of helping his mother with the visitors. The fact he was considered grown-up enough for the task filled him with pride. Áine was two years younger, but his mother always said she was 'mature beyond her years'. And yet, she had chosen him.

Outside, the visitor could be seen halfway up the field, his pace slow and unsteady. The hesitancy in his gait clear even from where they stood.

'Stay behind me as we approach,' she said, taking off towards the man. 'And try and get ahead of him once I start talking, alright? Stand yourself between him and the cliff – without getting too close to the edge, mind.'

'Okay,' he said, nerves betrayed by the sudden rise in his voice.

The man stopped long before they reached him. He was lost in ferocious thought, his finger striking out ahead of him, as if jabbing at some unseen person.

His mother used her phone voice that time: more formal and clipped than her real one. Posher, like she'd stripped the Tralee out of it. 'Excuse me, sir,' she said. 'Excuse me.' Micheál only heard it when she answered the phone in the hallway, or when he rang her at work, those first few moments before she knew it was him. It always gave him a twisted feeling in his stomach, hearing her speak to him as if he were a stranger.

The man turned, sheathing his finger by his side. The man was old enough, his mother's age; his nose was curved and had red veins around its tip. One side of the man's face was shaved, and a single clearing line had been drawn through the facial hair on his other side. The rest remained. It made him look off balance. Or maybe it was his eyes that made him appear that way, darting from side to side, not holding on to anything for more than a moment.

'You're looking for the Hegartys' place, are you?' his mother continued.

The man scratched at the unshaven part of his cheek. 'Sorry?'

'The Hegartys, sir, is that who you're looking for? You seem to have lost your way, though. They're a few houses further back, down the headland.'

The man turned towards the cliff edge, saw Micheál. A boy already the same height as him. Micheál breathed in, puffed up his chest. He wondered if he should reach for the man, tackle him. A part of him felt like a goalie, waiting to see if he could save an impending penalty.

The man's head dropped as he turned back to face Micheál's mother. 'The Hegartys, yes.' His hands linked behind him, right thumb digging into left palm. 'Is this not the right house?'

His mother smiled. 'I'm afraid not,' she said. 'But I can show you the way, if you'd like. Though maybe you should come inside for a cup of tea first? You look tired from all your walking.'

He took one last look at Micheál, the cliff. He seemed on the verge of crumpling in upon himself. 'I'd like that, yes.'

11

Sammy is rushing up and down the hallway before the gate's even open. Micheál only needs to open the door a fraction and he darts out, tail wagging. From the window, he watches the car climb towards the house. The kettle has boiled before Áine's out of the car. She gives the slightest knock, then bursts into the kitchen before he has a chance to answer, flinging her handbag and keys on the table.

'Can I use the jacks?' she asks.

'You don't need to ask.'

By the time she returns to the kitchen he has the tea on the table. Some biscuits, too (Kimberleys, her favourite). His grandfather had crafted the table, supposedly; the wood traded from a neighbour in return for his help one harvest. Even in his older years, his grandfather had been a strong man. Micheál's mother said his hands had been gnarled, immense, as though they too had been carved from wood. She used to keep a paisley-patterned cloth over the table, but he likes the wood, feels no need to keep it hidden.

Áine sits opposite him at the table. Micheál sips his tea, notices that she's starting to match him for greys. She takes a biscuit from the packet and bites a chunk out of it.

'The drive down was okay?'

'Fine. I took that bypass around Macroom; it's a real time-saver.'

'It's meant to be, alright.'

Áine finishes her biscuit. Sammy moves closer to her, searching the floor for crumbs.

'Ryan is feeling better? The chickenpox?'

'He's getting there, though I wish I could tie him up, at times. He won't stop scratching, the cheeky pup. If he ends up marking that beautiful face of his, I'll kill him.'

Micheál smiles. A memory returns to him of his own bout of chickenpox. How he'd been quarantined in his bedroom for the first few days. His mother dabbing calamine lotion on to his spots with cotton wool, the temporary relief. How his sisters had lingered at his window, and he'd sometimes hidden underneath the sill, before popping up, roaring. They would run away, screaming, only to creep back, giggling, waiting for the reappearance of their monster brother.

'I was sorry to hear about Nadine,' she says, eyes fixed on him, examining his reaction to her name. 'Though I suppose enough time has passed by now for it not to be much of a surprise.'

He tries to keep his expression neutral. 'What about her?'

'The engagement.'

'Oh right.'

'You hadn't heard?'

He shakes his head.

'She posted it on Facebook.'

'You know I'm not on that anymore.' He pushes the plate of biscuits towards her, keeps his eyes on the plate as he waits for her to speak.

Áine takes another biscuit. He can feel the squint of grey eyes on him. Watching for a sign as to how he's taking the news. No doubt remembering how he was after Nadine left, the state into which he fell.

'Listen, Mick, I was chatting to Saoirse last weekend.'

'Oh yeah, how is she?'

'You know her. Happy out. They've offered her more hours in the school in Seoul she's working in, but she's still thinking of moving on after Christmas. Maybe trying China this time.'

'Oh good; that'd be an experience, I'd say.'

'Anyway, she mentioned the selling-up idea again, Mick.'

'Oh yeah?'

'Yeah. It just seems like the right time now, d'you know?'

'I could see that, alright, I suppose.'

Áine's fingernail taps against the enamel cup with enough force to chip cup or nail. 'Mick, Saoirse and I both want this. We need it, really, what with her travels and Brian being put back to part-time at the factory. Damien is starting school next year, as you know.'

'I do.'

Micheál is surprised when his sister's hand rests atop his. 'We all need to be rid of this place, Mick; it's not doing us any good.'

He looks away from her, towards the dog. Something about Sammy's sprawled-out position on the floor, he thinks, suggests a bone-deep tiredness.

XII

Micheál ran around the mowed section of grass by the gable end of the house, hurley in hand. 'And it's Burns for Kerry now approaching the sliotar, minutes left in this All-Ireland final.' Ash slipped under leather and lifted it into the air; then, in one smooth motion, he swung the hurley and struck the sliotar at the side of the house, already spotted beyond redemption. 'At least this wall doesn't face the road,' his mother often said. Behind him, Saoirse sat amid a flattened circle of wildflowers, talking to herself.

The sliotar hits the upper, triangular section of the wall much closer to the attic window than he'd planned. He'd never hear the end of it if he broke it again. He caught the falling sliotar, pivoted. 'And Burns has pulled Kerry level as we enter time added on. One more chance for the Ballyheigue man now to snatch a historic win for the Kingdom.'

A snort came from the side of the house. Áine stood, leaning against the wall. 'Have Kerry even ever won a hurling All-Ireland?' she asked.

'Yeah, they have,' he countered, his face burning at being caught commentating on his own imaginary game. He left out that the year Kerry last won a hurling All-Ireland was 1892.

'What do you want?' he asked, smacking the sliotar hard against the wall, close to her. She remained where she was, a smirk on her face. He thought about hitting it again, even closer to her this time, though, whatever about the attic window, he knew he'd be killed if he hit her with the sliotar. Still, he desperately wanted to aim it close, just to get her to flinch or jump even a little.

The look she gave him next was one he didn't recognise.

A screech from behind them. A jolt of fear pitched through Micheál, but when he spun around, he saw that it was a cry of delight from Saoirse, as she conversed with the land or creatures or maybe even ghosts around her. He recalled his mother saying, not unkindly, 'That one's away with the fairies.'

'What was it like?' Áine asked in a quieter voice.

Micheál swung the hurley at some daisies in the grass, scythed them. 'What was what like?'

She sighed. 'Helping Mam with the visitor.'

In that moment, Micheál realised what that look from her

had meant. She was jealous. She couldn't stand that their mother had picked him. For all the praise she got, all the test results and her reports and the ways that Áine seemed to be their mother's favourite – despite all of this, she had chosen him. And this infuriated her.

He slapped the sliotar against the wall, far away from Áine this time. Then he pucked it into the air, jumped up and caught it as it fell. The hard leather stung his palm, but he was used to the sensation. Áine moved towards him, freckled nose scrunched up in a way it tended to when she was particularly annoyed. 'Well?' she asked.

He shrugged. 'It was fine. Easy. Mam said I'm a natural,' he added, lying.

He struck the sliotar into the air again, and from the look on Áine's face he knew that she was hoping it would crash down on his head and knock him dead.

13

Sammy's whining brings him out of it, the daze he's been in since Áine left – since she mentioned the word 'sell', really. Or maybe it was 'engagement'. He glances up at the clock from where he sits at the kitchen table, the signs of Áine's visit still unmoved before him: the remnants of tea in both cups, the soda bread and butter, the half-eaten packet of Kimberleys. Sammy had long since cleared any crumbs from the floor.

'Sorry,' Micheál says, rising. 'I'll get the dinner on now, don't worry.'

A blast of sourness strikes him as soon as he opens the fridge, which he had decided not to clean during his spree, figuring Áine was unlikely to look inside during her visit. Ignoring the smell, he takes out the packet of chicken fillets and places it on the sideboard by the gas cooker. What'll he have with them? For a moment he is unable to think of anything; he's not even sure of his options.

Áine had left shortly after she said what she'd come to say. He asked if she wanted to remain for dinner at least, but she said she really needed to get back. She had a long drive ahead. 'You'll think about it, anyway?' she asked at the door, the bay unusually placid behind her.

'I will, I will.'

At her car, they hesitated, unsure how to part. He moved in for a hug at first, but thought he spotted something in her eyes that discouraged this, though the moment he pulled back, Áine leaned in. The whole thing left them both hovering, buffeted. He felt his face burn as he held out a hand. 'Give my best to the family.'

She took his hand and, with a rueful smile, said, 'I will, Mick. And stay safe, you hear me?'

As soon as his food is cooked and plated – baby potatoes and frozen peas to go with the chicken – he pours a healthy portion of dog food into Sammy's bowl. It's silly, Micheál knows, but he likes for them to eat their dinner together.

Afterwards, as he washes the ware, he looks out the window above the sink. Overcast, but still dry. He feels that restlessness in him that comes on when he's been inside too long, and senses the same energy in Sammy, his tail slashing from side to side. There should be enough daylight left for a walk.

Outside, Micheál trundles down to the front gate and out on to the road. Sammy turns left ahead of him, heading north. He knows the way. They follow the road for half a mile before their destination comes into view, back off the road to the direct west: the remains of the promontory fort, Cahercarbery More, set at the end of the headland, where he used to play with Tuan and Stephen. This is where Micheál goes on the days that he doesn't venture into Ballyheigue. It is important to allow himself one daily excursion; otherwise, he figures, he'd soon go over the cliffs himself.

The trek to the fort from the road is longer than it appears, about half a mile over uneven rocky terrain pocketed with ferns, nettles. Not much of the fort remains now, bar a low stone wall raised on a bank, with some hut sites built inside the wall. A couple of trenches remain visible, and a causeway leading into the fort's interior from the east.

Micheál steps inside the ruin and sits on cold stone, staring out to sea. The last time the three of them were at the fort was shortly after Micheál first helped his mother. He had been desperate to tell them about the visitor. How he'd helped save him. His life. His soul. He felt like a hero, but one who had to keep his heroism a secret. 'Like a superhero,' his mother had said when he complained about not being able to tell anyone. 'Like Christopher Reeve.'

'You mean Clark Kent? As in Superman?'

'Yes, sorry, love. You need to be Clark Kent with them, so you can be Superman for me. You see that, don't you?'

'I suppose,' he muttered, gaze shifting to the sea below. It was rough, the colour of lead. Not even Superman could see through that.

Micheál and Sammy make it back to the house just ahead of a shower skirting in off the bay. He turns on the TV and sits down on the couch. Enough light still comes in the window to see the rise up to the house, the wrought-iron gate, the road that loops around both sides of the headland. Hard to miss any movement from this vantage point.

The daze that had come over him after Áine's visit is starting to give way to something else now – a tumult, in his stomach, his chest. The whole thing is spinning around in him; he won't know for certain how he feels until everything has stilled.

He has always been like this at such moments. He remembers fights with Nadine, particularly in their early years together in college in Limerick. How in the breathless rush of their arguing, he'd often lose his place, the tenuous thread of his righteousness. *No. I didn't say that. No. That's not what I meant.* It'd be hours later, when he was often by himself, before he strung everything back together. Knew exactly what he'd wanted to say. And now she's engaged.

Rain comes in and night soon follows. The TV has little to offer, but his mind is not in the right state for reading – and he is almost through his latest batch from the mobile library, anyway – so he flicks until he lands on a *Friends* rerun. The One That I Have Seen a Zillion Times. It's what he's looking for, though: something light, something to distract. Still, every few minutes, his gaze drifts to the window. Darkness, rain, the occasional burst of headlights. Other than that, nothing.

He must be on the fourth or fifth episode when Sammy whines by the door. Micheál rises with a grunt, his lower back stiff. 'Alright, lad, I'm coming.' Rain pelts the front of the house as he opens the door enough to allow Sammy to slink outside. Rain sneaks in, spattering the tiles, the counter beside the door, as he waits for the dog to finish his business. He is taking his time. Has he caught a scent? Headed up towards the cliffs? But when he sticks his head outside, Sammy is bounding towards him, eager for shelter.

Door closed, he sits back in front of the TV. And realises that his mind has finally stilled. He has caught up with how he feels.

Áine will not be happy.

PART TWO

14

A sound wakes him to darkness. Micheál props himself up on his elbows, listens. It had been an actual sound this time, he is sure of it. There. A cough. He brings a fist to his mouth so as not to answer it with one of his own. It's better to come on them by surprise, to give them as little time as possible to consider how his arrival impacts on their plans. Reaching for crumpled jeans on the floor, he thinks how every year is the same; the lead-up to Christmas always brings them.

XV

For several years, Micheál's weekdays began and ended on a rusted, damp-smelling bus that took him, Tuan and Stephen from Ballyheigue into Tralee. Their new school, the Christian Brothers Secondary School – known as 'The Green' due to its location beside the town park – was the bus's last stop after Balloonagh, Moyderwell and the Presentation, the other schools in town.

The three friends stuck together as much as possible that

first year, taking many of the same subjects, and meeting for lunch every day. They'd walk into town during the forty-five-minute break to buy sweets and loiter in the square, watching the older students smoke, sneaking glances at the girls from the Presentation and Balloonagh. No one played hurling in town – it was all football. The school didn't even have a hurling team. They asked their PE teacher, Mr Hanlon, about the possibility of setting up a hurling team, but he declared that there wouldn't be enough interest. He was rumoured to be an Aston Villa fan. 'Who the fuck supports Villa?' Tuan wondered, incredulous. Twice a week, they brought their gear in so they could go to training back in Ballyheigue straight after school, the sight of their hurleys drawing derisory comments: 'Go on back to Kilkenny, you pricks.' One day Micheál returned to the classroom after lunch to find his hurley splintered beside his desk. It looked like it had been smacked against something tough, likely the old boundary wall behind the prefabs. Stephen insisted that an attack on one of them was an attack on them all, and they spent several bus rides planning their revenge, before sneaking into the empty classroom to spill Tippex into the likely culprit's bag, a brick-headed townie called Deano.

Micheál didn't fit in at school, but at least his friendship with Tuan and Stephen, and the hurling, gave him a sense of himself away from the house, from the secret work he undertook, and from the feeling that he could be called upon at any time to go out on to the cliffs.

His mother had told him that there'd be, on average, about seven a year – though one year there had been as many as twelve. That first year after his father's death turned out to be a quiet time: after the 'lost' man's visit, only two more came. And both were dealt with easily enough. After each visit, his mother pointed out mistakes he'd made and instructed him on how to best deal with the visitors. Listen. Never interrupt them – they need to be able to tell that you're listening. Try to build rapport. Use open body language. Never judge them. Be patient and kind. And always look for the hook.

16

He brings the boy, Luke McCarthy, down from the cliff with the first lightening of the sky to the east, the wind vanes atop the Stack Mountains taking form on the horizon with cyclical salutes. Micheál walks a step behind him, ready should the red-haired seventeen-year-old change his mind and make again for the break in land. But the boy is all hunch and earth-focused eyes now, his earlier frenzied determination gone, so Micheál shepherds him with ease towards the house.

Inside, Micheál pulls a chair out from the kitchen table, the one facing away from the door. The boy sits on the offered chair, his hands buried up his sleeves. Sammy rests on the tiled floor beside him, tongue out, and the boy stares absently at him. Sammy had been great throughout the night. He'd gotten close to the boy before Micheál managed to make any sort of connection, lying beside him in the sodden grass, licking his hand, resting his head on the boy's thigh.

Micheál walks to the couch and the blankets spread over the back of it. Two of the warmest he puts around the boy's shoulders, the other he wraps around himself. It had remained dry while they were outside, but it had been bitter, a proper winter night. The boy had come surprisingly prepared for the weather: waterproofs on, Garter boots, gloves. It took a while before he was ready to talk. Micheál did not rush him. The boy explained how he'd told his parents that he was going for a hike, something he'd been doing regularly in recent weeks. So they wouldn't worry for a few hours, at least. 'I didn't know where I was going, really, though; all I wanted was the sea. But when I got to Ballyheigue, it didn't feel right, so I kept walking, until I got here. Until there was no more land to walk.'

The kettle grumbles to a boil. Luke has noticed the portrait of Christ, his gazed fixed on the blinking red heart. Micheál keeps meaning to get rid of it; he is unsure why he hasn't yet taken it down.

'How do you take your tea?' Micheál asks.

The boy continues to stare at the exposed heart.

'Luke?'

He starts. 'Black, black is fine.'

Micheál places the cup of tea in front of the boy, who doesn't drink from it, but holds the cup in short bursts, the heat likely too much for his sensitive skin to endure for long. The boy's gaze still shies away from him. Most of the conversation up on the cliff had been like this – eyes either turned away or lowered to the space between them.

After another spell of cup-holding, he asks in a timorous voice, 'Is it okay if I close my eyes for a minute? Maybe on the couch, or even if I could just put my head down here on the table?'

Micheál stands. 'I've a spare room. Here, let me show you.'

The visitors' room had belonged to Saoirse, though she was moved into Áine's room whenever a visitor needed it. This was usually on the night of a visit, or the early morning after-wards, when his mother brought the visitors into the house after they'd been turned. She didn't like the idea of them leaving too soon, felt there'd be too strong a chance that they'd go to another part of the headland and jump, or just walk into the sea by Meenogahane Pier or Ballyheigue. So she invited them in. Offered food, tea, water. Asked if they would like to pray, if there was anyone she could call. And, in some cases, she offered them the bed. 'When the night passes, things will seem different,' she often said. 'Hope comes with the morning light.' Most of the time the visitors left after a few hours. Sometimes, though, they stayed for a day or two, spending most of their time in the bedroom, sleeping, crying, staring at the pink, seashell-patterned walls, or ignoring the offerings brought to them: cups of tea, quartered chicken sandwiches, biscuits or fizzy drinks left over from Christmas. The longest stay was by a man from Castleisland called Johnny King. He lingered for a week after he was brought down from the cliff. An out-of-work electrician, he spent most of that week checking and double-checking every light switch and socket in the house, ensuring everything was in working order. 'It's just his way of saying thank you,' his mother explained after he'd left. 'For saving him.'

Luke lies down on the bed, which Micheál always keeps freshly dressed. The boy turns away, curling into a foetal shape. He is still shivering, so Micheál takes the blanket off

49

his own shoulders and rests it over him. 'Get a bit of rest there, Luke. You'll be surprised the difference it'll make.'

'Okay.'

Micheál returns to the kitchen and finishes his tea, sitting on the seat the boy vacated. Sammy has already fallen asleep beside him, a low whine as he dreams, the occasional leg kick. Micheál tiptoes back to the visitors' room, listens. The deep, regular cadence of sleep. Good. He takes Luke's phone out of his jacket pocket. By the time the boy had opened up to him on the cliff, they'd been sitting close enough for Micheál to see the numbers he keyed into his phone as he showed him one of the threads on Messenger. Micheál tapped in the code. Eighteen missed calls from Home. Twelve missed calls from Mam. Seven from Dad. Several messages:

Where r u?
Ring home asap
Luke, let us know where u r!

Micheál dials Home.

Half an hour later, the boy's parents arrive in a twelve-year-old maroon Ford Mondeo that struggles up the incline to the house in the wrong gear, the engine whining. They park by the front door, Mrs McCarthy opening her door while the car is still moving. Behind the car, the bay is cast in cobalt, Brandon Point to the south-west lost to rain.

Mrs McCarthy steps out of the car and Micheál sees that the boy has found himself with much of her appearance: the red hair, pale complexion, slender frame. Where his voice had been halting and timid, though, hers is forceful. 'Where is he?' she asks, half-accusatory, as if he has brought the boy to this point. Only the slightest hint of panic in her eyes betrays her bullishness. Mr McCarthy emerges from the driver's seat, his ruddy, furrowed face confirmation of a life spent mostly outdoors. The way he worries the keys in his hand makes Micheál think of his mother and her rosary beads.

'Come inside,' he says. 'And be quiet, please. He's sleeping.'

As Micheál makes a fresh batch of tea, Sammy moves between both McCarthys, who now sit at the kitchen table. They stare at the tea Micheál places before them with a distant, stumped gaze. They look exhausted, and Micheál knows that the deep tiredness they feel is coming for him too; in many ways he's surprised it hasn't arrived yet.

'He was always a morose child,' Mrs McCarthy says.

'Not like this, Helen,' Mr McCarthy responds.

'Do you remember his thing with the dog?'

'I know, love, I know, but this is different.' He looks to Micheál. 'Did he tell you anything? About why he, you know, wanted to do that?'

Micheál takes the boy's phone from his pocket. He feels a slight twang of guilt for showing them the boy's messages without his permission, but Luke has gotten to this point by not telling anyone what has been happening. They need to know, if they are to help him.

He opens the app, scrolls down. 'This is just one of the threads,' he says, handing the phone to the McCarthys. 'But there are more of them. Then there are the texts and voicemails – and that's just outside of school. From the little he told me, it sounds like it's even worse at the school itself.

Either way, he hasn't had any escape from it for a few months. And for a while now, I think, it has felt like he couldn't go on with it anymore.'

'Jesus,' Mr McCarthy whispers. 'He never said anything, not a word.'

Mrs McCarthy shakes her head. 'He has been especially quiet lately, but I thought it just had to do with him being in Leaving Cert year.'

'He wants to do a film course up in Dublin,' Mr McCarthy says to Micheál.

Micheál nods. 'He told me.'

Early on, during their time up on the cliff, Micheál had gone through a number of topics in an attempt to forge a connection. He had rambled about how he'd hated school, what sort of things he got for Christmas when he was the boy's age, how he once got dumped during Christmas holidays – which wasn't true, but boys often overreacted when they had their heart broken for the first time. Nothing registered. It was only when listing his favourite Christmas movies – *The Muppet Christmas Carol*, *It's a Wonderful Life*, *Die Hard* – that the boy turned to him and said, '*Die Hard* is not a Christmas movie.' That, of all things, was the hook.

'What do we do?' Mrs McCarthy asks.

'Well, first off, he needs someone to talk to – someone who's not me, or you.' The couple exchange glances. 'Also, from what he told me about the school, you probably need to get him out of there, at least for a while. Or move him to another school altogether.'

A squeak from the hallway – the visitors' room door opening. He intentionally never oils it.

'I want to go home,' Luke says, rubbing his eyes. He looks much younger than his seventeen years in that moment.

Both parents stand. His mother goes to him, embraces him. His father's face pales, as if only now registering what has happened. In a rasp of a voice, he says, 'That's no problem, son. Let's all go home right now.'

XVII

It was the middle of the day, a Saturday. Micheál, at hurling training in Ballyheigue, missed the visitor's arrival. When he returned home, he saw his mother and an old, suited man up by the cliff. He hopped off his bike, dropped his hurley, gear-bag and helmet on the ground, and broke into a run. His mother flung him a look as he approached, one that seemed to say: *What took you so long?* His eyes dropped to wildflowers for a moment, then rose with determination to the old man, dressed in a navy tweed suit and newly polished black loafers. A matching hat called a homburg. 'I'm sorry,' the man said to his mother, before Micheál had time to sneak behind him, block his route to the cliff edge, 'but I really must go.' As if late for a train or an appointment. 'I can't keep her waiting any longer.'

And with that he was gone.

Micheál clearly remembers him doffing his hat to his mother, just before, but she later said that never happened; he'd simply put his hand to it, to secure it and make sure it stayed in place as he fell. 'He wanted to look his best for her,' she said. 'She'd loved that hat, apparently; had bought it for him for one of their anniversaries.'

Afterwards, she led Micheál into the kitchen, set him down at the table as she made the necessary call to Adrian Spring at the station. Micheál trembled, the occasional sob heaving his chest. His sisters watched on from the hallway, Saoirse half-hiding behind Áine. His mother reached into the press beside the fridge, pulled out a bottle of Jameson and poured him his first whiskey. He knows now that it was a double, at least.

'Drink that,' she said. 'Slowly, mind; only sip at it.'

He winced and coughed as it scoured his throat.

His mother sat opposite him, rested linked hands on the table. She waited until he'd met her gaze before speaking. 'Sometimes they're too far gone to be saved, Micheál. It's not our fault. We can only do our best, do you understand?'

With watery eyes, he nodded.

'Say it.'

'We can only do our best.'

'Good boy.'

18

Mid-morning, he gets the ladder hook, pulls down the Stira attic stairs from the hallway ceiling, and climbs. Once on timber panelling, Micheál moves, hunched over, towards the attic's sole window: a square-shaped opening at waist height that allows a view of the wildflower field, cliffs and a portion of the bay in the direction of the Maharees and Brandon Point.

Beneath the window rests the orange-and-yellow-spotted single mattress that had been used on his bed until he was seven, maybe eight. He'd liked it because the colours reminded him of Garfield. Beside the mattress stands a squat, mahogany bedside table, another cast-off that had found its way to the attic. Equipment decorates the table: binoculars, field guide, camera and notebook, a bag of mixed nuts.

He lies front-down on the mattress. Out the window, clouds hang dark and heavy; Micheál can tell that they will soon burst. He scans his field of vision with his naked eye, sees nothing, not even by the feeders at the border of the long grass. Lifting the binoculars to his eyes, he tries again. He slowly searches the field; the birds can often be difficult to see in the long grass, never mind identify. He checks the rockier terrain up by the cliffs, adjusts the magnification as he looks to sea. Nothing. He reaches for the nuts and starts into them.

Behind him, water pools in the tank, which is itself lost from sight behind the clutter. There are cardboard boxes marked in his mother's writing: 'Photo Albums 1988–92', 'Áine Primary Copybooks', 'Saoirse Art/Sheet Music'. Then there are the unboxable items: the stomach curler his mother had gotten his father one Christmas as a joke, the old TV, his father's set of Titleist golf clubs, the tennis rackets they used to bring to the beach, three broken clocks. Something about the clocks comforts him; the idea of time being broken time and time again. Sometimes, when leaving the attic, he will go to one of the clocks – a blue-and-white porcelain dish with the dial etched on it in Roman numerals; it had been a wedding gift to his parents from an unremembered relative – and move the delicate hands until they match the time on his phone. Only then does he feel able to descend.

His phone begins to vibrate. He removes it from his jeans pocket, looks at the screen. Áine. This is her fourth call in the last two days. She had kept her distance the first few weeks after her visit, allowing him time to mull over what she'd said, her ultimatum, as he now refers to it, if only in his head. When they next spoke, he sidestepped the topic, saying he needed more time to think. That worked until a couple of weeks ago, when she made it clear that she wanted an answer when they next spoke. He waits for the phone to ring out, and tosses it on to the mattress.

A flurry of movement outside. He picks up the binoculars. Two birds that look like finches adorn the seed-filled feeder. Too pale to be goldfinches, about the same size as a chaffinch. If they'd stay still for a moment, he'd be able to place them. There. That's it. Glossy black head, washed with brown. Yellow bill. The orange throat and chest are the giveaway. Two bramblings. Both adult males, he thinks, though it's difficult to tell apart the winter male from the winter female. Neither seem to have the grey-brown colouring on their head, though, the telltale sign of the female. Micheál turns to the table, jots the sighting in his notebook. When he looks back outside, the birds have gone.

XIX

Áine's voice carried from the hallway to his bedroom. 'Micheál, it's for you.'

Micheál put the book he was reading for school, *Goodnight Mister Tom*, down beside him on the bed. The landline sat on a wicker desk in the hallway, a notepad and biro beside it in case note-taking was required. The receiver lay on its side, cord twirled around itself, knotted.

'Hello?'

Tuan's voice. 'Where were you?'

'What?'

'Hurling training this morning. How many have you missed now, Mick? You're going to lose your place in the team if you keep this up.'

Micheál had not gone to the hurling since the old man jumped, his mother's words resounding in his head. *We can only do our best.* She had not repeated those words, but he still felt them. Was he trying his best if he wanted to stay over at Steven's or Tuan's house one night instead of remaining home? Was he trying his best if he went to hurling training two nights a week, and played a game on Saturdays? With each thought he felt the knuckled pressure of her disappointment in between his shoulder blades. What if a poor soul came during one of these absences and she was unable to deal with the visitor by herself? Or what if a visitor was violent, or if she were forced to rope in one or both of his sisters to help? Would it be worth it? The quick game of hurling, the sleepover, the unnecessary cycle into the village. Could he do all that and honestly say that he was doing his best?

'Mam's going into Tralee this afternoon and she said she'll pick me up a video in Xtra-vision,' Tuan said. 'You want to call over and watch it later? I've already said it to Stephen.'

Micheál wrapped the phone cord around his index finger, the skin whitening where the cord tightened. 'I can't, sorry.'

'Fine, so,' Tuan said, hanging up.

His mother's voice reached out from the kitchen: 'Micheál, can you set the table for me, please? Lunch is ready.'

20

A terrified Santa decorates the shop window, razor-toothed reindeer chasing him across the pane; above his head, a white-bubbled wail of 'Ho, no, no!' Chuckling, Micheál steps inside.

'Festive, right?' Brenda says, guessing the source of his mirth. A slender gold band of tinsel brows the cash register.

'Poor Santa,' he responds.

'Ah, he had it coming. As my mam used to say, who is Santa but another fat man hoarding all the good stuff? Why should we be happy getting something off him once a year when he gets to keep everything for himself the rest of the time?'

'A wise woman, your mother.'

Brenda shrugs. 'In some ways.'

The shop is quieter than normal, so much so that he can hear a TV that she must have left on in the flat upstairs. It takes him a moment to realise the cause.

'Radio broken?'

'No, I just needed a break from all that Christmas music. If I have to hear Mariah Carey screech what she wants for Christmas one more time . . .'

'Fair enough.'

She leans forward, elbows on the counter. 'You hear about Pat Hennessy?'

'What about him?'

'He sold the sheep and has got himself a new herd, but you'll never guess what they are.'

'What are they?'

'Guess.'

'But you said I'd never guess.'

'I know, but at least take one guess before I tell you.'

'He take some Friesians in?'

Brenda scoffs. 'No, you're miles off.'

'Go on, so, tell me.'

She's nearly over the counter to him by now: 'Llamas.'

'What, llamas? Are you serious?'

'Llamas, I'm telling you. Fucking llamas. He did it all without consulting Maire, too, so it's likely that he's out sleeping with them now on top of all that.'

Micheál laughs as he collects the last few items on his list: the pound of Kerrygold butter, slices of ham, toothpaste. He has so many questions, like did Hennessy mean to buy llamas? Or did he confuse them with alpacas, whose fleeces you can at least sell? He is about to ask as much when a man's voice comes from the narrow hallway, the one that leads to the storage room and the stairs to her flat.

'Who is it, Junior?'

A rainbowed curtain of beads blocks Micheál's view of the hallway, but he recognises the voice, has time to mask his surprise before the beads part and Aengus Dillane appears. From the shape of him, all shoulder and arms, you wouldn't think he'd given up the hurling three years ago. Micheál tries to straighten his posture as he holds out a hand, braces to match a more-than-firm handshake.

'You're well, Aengus?'

'Ah, Mick, good to see you.'

The handshake is just about a draw.

'How's Cork going?'

'I'm actually back down here now, would you believe. Got some work in Tralee, and keep it to yourself but it looks like I'm getting the coaching role for Ballyheigue in the new year.'

'Oh right, fair play. What about Dan?'

'His wife's ill, apparently, so he feels like he can't give the time needed to the club. I'd been offered the job in Tralee just a week before the club approached me. Funny how these things work out, isn't it?'

'It is, alright.'

Brenda scans Micheál's groceries and bags them. As she hands him his change, she meets his gaze. 'Here, answer the phone the next time Áine rings, would you?'

Caught off guard, he scowls and turns away.

'Good seeing you, Mick,' Aengus says. 'Have a good Christmas.'

'You too,' he says, already half out the door.

Once on his bike, he pedals furiously out of town, struggling against a stiff south-westerly. So, Aengus is back. It had seemed like they'd finally broken up for good three years ago. He'd gone off the rails when dropped from the Kerry squad. As if it were that big a thing. It was the Kerry hurlers, for fuck sake; Sammy could play hurling for Kerry. Brenda and Aengus had never seemed like that great a match – one of those couples who got together too young and settled, figured that what was good was good enough when there was no guarantee of better. Jesus, this wind. By the time Micheál reaches the primary school, he's spent, and not yet even halfway home.

XXI

He was swimming in the sea, out near Illauntannig, when she woke him. The waking did not feel so much like a lifting out of the water, but a hand around his ankle, dragging him down. She was by the foot of the bed, raincoat and boots already on.

'Come on, I think there's someone out there.'

In his stomach was a frenzy, a bird realising too late that it lay on the wrong side of a window. 'I don't feel good,' he muttered lamely. It was all he could think to say. He wanted to stay there, in bed, away from the place where people fell. Just tipped their hats and disappeared. This situation was real now in a way that it hadn't been before. 'Real.' It was the wrong word; he knew that. But it was the one that came to mind as he lay there, his mother looking down on him in the half-light.

She turned and walked out into the hallway. 'Your coat and boots are in the kitchen. Hurry.'

As her rushed steps retreated down the hallway, Micheál knew that he had no choice but to follow her.

22

Sergeant Adrian Spring sits at the kitchen table, cup of tea and plate of Kimberleys placed before him. He is wearing his uniform, though he had driven out here in his personal car, a decade-old silver Toyota Corolla, rather than the squad car. Likely a desire for discretion, Micheál presumes. Not wanting to draw eyes.

Spring slurps the tea, takes another biscuit, working his way through the pile diligently. 'Some weather, eh? Santa will get blown miles off course, the way it's going.'

Micheál nods. 'Rudolph will be needed, alright.'

Unnoticed by Spring, crumbs fall on his light-blue shirt and navy tie. His eyes struggle to meet Micheál's; he seems to like the distraction of the food. The sergeant has always had trouble coming here; though, to be fair to him, he makes the trip once or twice every year from the station in the village – even though it'd be more accurate to call the squat, pebble-dashed bungalow on the Tralee road an outpost, what with the district headquarters in Listowel and divisional headquarters in Tralee. He comes out to 'touch base', as he puts it. He'd been doing it for years now, since Micheál was a child. His personal phone number is one of those Micheál's mother wrote on the list taped inside the kitchen cupboard for emergencies. He is the contact point on the rare instances when the coastguard helicopter or RNLI lifeboat is needed, or if someone has to be taken in for their own protection.

The conversation always steps along the same well-worn path – the weather, hurling, the Premiership – as Spring skirts the real reason for the visit as long as he can. It isn't till the tea is finished and biscuits eaten that he tends to hand Micheál the business card for the local councillor, Harry Holmes, an English 'blow-in', as Spring calls him, living in Causeway. The force would be happy to pay for any sessions, he is always told. What you're doing is tough. There is someone for you to talk to, if you need it. This time is no different, except the business card is new, cream in colour with an almost gritty texture. Dr Joanne Twomey. Clinical psychologist. Her office has a Tralee address.

'What happened to Harry?'

'Decided to blow out back to England.'

'Oh right?'

Spring shrugs, still munching. 'Missed the homeland too much, apparently.'

Micheál looks at the card again, hands it back to the sergeant. 'Thanks for the offer, but it's still a no. I'm fine.'

'Well, have you at least thought any more about letting us put up a barrier of some sort by the cliffs, or a sign, or even a phone? It could make a difference. And the Pieta crowd have an office in Tralee now; they could likely even get some people out here the odd night, maybe help carry the load, d'you know?'

Micheál feels a heat build in him, but keeps it from his voice. 'Sure there's no need. I'm always here for them.'

Spring shakes his head. 'Just like your mother. Well, look, the offer's there if you change your mind.'

Task completed, the sergeant rubs his palms along the thighs of his navy trousers, stands. They shake hands at the door, the chill wind making both of them tense. Micheál has long since forgotten the name of Spring's wife, so says, 'Give my season's greetings to herself and the rest of the family.'

'Same to you and yours,' Spring replies, running for his car. When Micheál begins clearing off the kitchen table, he sees that Spring has left the card tucked under his saucer. A new tactic, that, Micheál thinks, as he tears it to pieces.

XXIII

One weekend, when Micheál was fourteen, his mother bought him a TV for his bedroom. It was a boxy Sharp with a twelve-inch screen, a fuzzy picture and flimsy antenna, but it was his. It came with a £20 VHS player from Dunnes Stores and a six-pack of blank tapes. He knew it was a bribe of sorts, an attempt at appeasement, so he would keep helping with the visitors. He didn't care. He had a TV in his room. Who else did he know that had their own TV? Well, Rian Gleeson in his class, but his father was a surgeon in the Bons Secours Hospital.

With only the two terrestrial channels available, RTÉ 1 and Network 2, there was often nothing to watch. This was where the blank tapes came in handy. Three tapes were set aside to record sport: *The Sunday Game*, Irish soccer internationals, the US Masters; one tape had the most recent episode of shows like *Friends*, *90210*, *The Simpsons*, *Veronica's Closet* and *Father Ted*. The two final tapes were for films.

Áine was furious about the TV set. She blew up one evening over dinner, saying it was unfair, asking why she and Saoirse had not been given one. Saoirse grunted an agreement, index fingernail in mouth, a habit their mother had tried, and failed, to break. Micheál wondered why she was getting involved. Saoirse hardly ever watched TV, anyway; had no time for it, always burrowed away in her bedroom, sketching, drawing, painting. Even though she was still in primary school, she'd decided that she was going to art college.

His mother stared at Áine, replied in a neutral tone: 'He's the eldest. Your turn will come when he moves out.' Something about the way she said that made his chest tighten.

Áine tried again. 'But, Mam –'

His mother held up a finger, eyes narrowing.

End of.

As each tape only had three hours' worth of recording, Micheál sometimes sat by the TV, hitting stop during the ad breaks, record when the show resumed. He would play an episode or movie again and again until he could practically recite it. He watched *Jurassic Park* at least a hundred times. *Reservoir Dogs* too, though he never told his mother, as he knew she'd think it far too violent. Same went with the thirty-odd minutes at the end of one of the film tapes that he filled with scenes from *Body Heat* and *About Last Night*, taped late at night with the sound on mute.

Sometimes he acted out scenes from the action movies he'd memorised, jumping off the bed-turned-electric-wire, crawling across the floor to avoid gunfire, smoking an imaginary cigarette. These movies, and shows, were all he had for company. Even Tuan and Stephen had stopped talking to him by then. Neither had taken it well, his leaving the hurling team and not wanting to hang out with them after school anymore – particularly as he could not give them a reason why. Both started to sit far away from him on the bus and blanked him altogether at school. Over time, Stephen took it further, calling him names from the back of the classroom, writing 'gay' and 'freak' in his copybooks.

One day, in English class, Mr O'Flaherty was scribbling Shakespeare on the blackboard when something smacked into the back of Micheál's head. Everyone behind him started to laugh as he raised a hand to his hair, felt wetness, a mushiness, as if his head had been opened and he was leaking out of himself. He turned round, saw a pulpy orange rolling into the aisle between the desks.

The laughter stopped when Mr O'Flaherty strode forward and picked up the orange. 'Who threw this?' The vein on his forehead was already pulsing, the one that had earned him his nickname. Throbby Robbie.

'Who threw this?' he shouted again. All eyes were focused on their textbooks. He yanked Micheál from his desk with some force, as if all this was somehow his doing. 'Go wash up,' he ordered.

As he left, Micheál glanced towards Stephen. From the little smirk on his face, his cheeks flushed, Micheál knew it was him.

24

Once he and Sammy are fed, Micheál sits down with a heavy sigh on the couch. He looks out the window towards the road below, near lost in darkness, and, satisfied that there is no movement, he reaches for one of the books on the coffee table in front of the TV, part of his latest batch from the mobile library. Sammy lies curled on the rug, napping.

For the last couple of years, he's found himself drawn to local history, stories that go back further than living memory, ones that seem lost to the general community. Tonight he reads about the Danish Silvery Robbery of 1730. A ship, the *Golden Lion*, ran aground in the bay during a storm – likely around the same spot where he'd seen a tanker earlier today as it made for Fenit. The captain of this ship, Johan Heitman, received help from the then-occupier of Ballyheigue Castle, Sir Thomas Crosbie, along with other locals. The ship's crew were brought ashore, along with a cargo that included a large haul of gold. Crosbie grew sick from his efforts and died shortly afterwards. Then the gold went missing. The author theorises that Crosbie's wife, and some other local elites, stole it – perhaps Crosbie's widow even took it as a form of compensation for her husband's life. Either way, Heitman was forced to leave Ballyheigue empty-handed. The gold was never found, and some suggest that it's still buried somewhere on the castle's grounds.

Micheál looks up from the page, unable to see anything now in the darkness beyond the rain-spattered window. He wonders why it was called a silver robbery if it was gold that they stole; and where did the Danes come into it? But he also senses a truth: even if there had been gold buried in these parts, it was long gone.

His phone vibrates on the coffee table, startling him. There is no need to look at the screen to know who is calling. He remembers Brenda's words from his last visit to the shop. He reaches forward, sighing, and picks up the phone.

'Áine,' he greets.

'Mick, what the hell –'

'I know, I know.'

'You can't just be –'

'I know, Áine; I'm sorry.'

'Stop cutting across me, Mick; let me say what I want to say. I'm allowed to give out to you when you've been acting the maggot.'

Micheál raps his knuckle against the hardback, stays silent. He hears Áine, with effort, steady her breathing.

'So?' she asks.

'What's that?'

'Do you have a decision for me?'

He sighs. 'I don't know, Áine.'

'Look, Mick, okay, I've been thinking about it, and how about you meet me halfway, alright?' Her now-measured tone suggests she had been expecting a response like this, had prepared for it. 'How about we don't put the place up for sale – not officially, at least – but instead we just put some feelers out, see if there's any interest? So that way we're not committing to anything, but we're still getting a sense of the market? That sound okay to you?'

Sammy stirs on the rug, a hind leg kicking out.

'Maybe, I don't know.'

'Come on, Mick. Give me this. We can say it's my Christmas present.'

A hand rests against his forehead; thumb and middle finger find both temples and begin to massage. A sensation in his stomach: a peeling away of sorts. 'I suppose there's no harm in putting some feelers out.'

'Good man, Mick. You're a good man.'

He flinches at that, the way she says it.

XXV

One evening, during Fifth Year, Micheál decided to sneak out. He needed a night away. One night as a normal teenager.

He had heard lads at school talking. How there was going to be a big night out at The Casement, a rundown two-star hotel with a bar and nightclub, down by the coast between Ballyheigue and Ardfert, that coming Saturday. Way out like this, the hotel needed some means of attracting punters; the management's solution was to allow in anyone who bothered to travel out there, no questions asked about age. Teens from all over north Kerry took advantage, some coming from as far as Listowel and Ballybunion.

Micheál put on his good jeans and a black shirt, so the sweat stains from his cycling wouldn't be noticed. He hopped out his window, the TV blaring from the kitchen. *Kenny Live*. Sneaking around the side of the house, he was forced to pass Saoirse's bedroom. He kept low, but she was sitting at her desk under the window, sketching, and saw him right away.

She threw him a puzzled frown. He brought a finger to his lips and she lifted her eyes to the ceiling, shook her head. He knew that he could count on her, unlike Áine, to say nothing. Her only response came a few days later when she handed him a sheet of A4 paper, a portrait of that moment. She had brought out something pale and alien-like about his features, maybe even sinister, with a swirl of dark blues and greys and blacks around him. A feeling in him he could not quite place, he had bunched up the paper, let it fall from his palm into the bin in his room.

He waited until he was around the bend of the road before he turned on the lights on his bike. As he cycled in the headland, his palms turned sweaty on the handlebars. His mother could, and likely would, discover his absence at any moment. He knew no one going to the club – well, he knew some, but none of them considered him a friend. Still, at least for one night, he'd be away.

He locked his bike to a lamp post in the car park of the hotel, his stomach quaking. The scent of the sea was strong on the air, dunes visible as an undulating blackness underneath the lighter tone of the western sky. Small pockets of clubbers hung around the car park. A queue snaked its way to the nightclub entrance. It appeared to be moving fast, which he took as a good sign. He had no ID with him, just a £20 note.

Once inside, he ordered a Bulmers at the crowded bar, served to him in a plastic cup. Not seeing anyone he knew, he stayed at the bar, trying to appear nonchalant. He'd never been around so many girls his own age, all giggles, exposed flesh and a smell he'd later learn was fake tan. Most of the lads were ordering lager, so when he finished the cider he followed suit. Nirvana's 'Smells like Teen Spirit' came on and the dance floor, a wood-panelled, sawdusted square of space below the bar, began to fill. Lads, some with chests bared, formed circles on the dance floor, jumping up and down. A drink flew out of a plastic cup, drenching the lad next to him. He felt a strong urge to join one of those circles, shout along with the lyrics. Instead, he remained at the bar, took deep gulps of the lager.

'Micheál fucking Burns, is that you?'

When he turned around all he saw was a white shirt glowing in the disco lights. Then he took in the familiar face, cheeks flaring and eyes glazed.

'Tuan, how are you?' he asked.

Micheál hadn't seen him since he'd left The Green at the start of the year. His parents had moved him to the private school in Tralee where you were said to be guaranteed good points in the Leaving.

A massive hand on his shoulder – Tuan was already six foot four and likely to grow another few inches before he levelled out. When the growth spurt struck a couple of years ago, the bainisteoir had moved him to midfield. He'd become the team's star player, although, given that it was hurling, few outside of Ballyheigue cared.

'We don't even have to wear a uniform, Mick; it's class,' he said, having dragged Micheál outside to talk while he had a smoke. 'And the girls . . .' he trailed off. 'I'm not sure my parents had the right idea sending me to a mixed school for the first time in my life, if you know what I mean?'

He pulled a naggin out of his pocket, offered it to Micheál. 'Thanks,' he said, taking a chug. Tuan demanded he drink

71

the rest. 'You seem way behind everyone else here; you have some catching up to do. Come on, lad, it's time for some shots.'

Soon Micheál found himself bouncing around the dance floor with Tuan and his friends, the naggin finished, along with several rounds of shots – sambuca, tequila, Aftershock – most of which he hadn't bought. He jumped up and down, a taste of liquorice in his mouth, his mind a pleasurable fog.

'Guards!'

The shout came from nearby, then pinged around the club, panicked echoes rising above the music. Micheál looked towards the entrance, saw two Garda hats above the crowd. Tuan gestured for him to follow. He led him into a hallway to the right of the DJ box, passed snogging couples lining the walls to an already open fire exit. Outside, they sprinted across the field. Once they reached the dunes, Micheál bent over marram grass and vomited. Tuan laughed. 'Ah, lad, I didn't take you for such a lightweight.' Micheál felt better after vomiting; everything spun a little less.

They settled back in the dunes to wait until the squad car left. Tuan pulled a ten-pack of Benson & Hedges out of his pocket. 'Nicked them off my dad,' he said. 'He always blames my sister for taking them.' He laughed and offered one to Micheál, who shook his head. If he tried a cigarette now, he would only puke again.

'Look, Mick, I just want to say that I'm sorry about what happened. With the bus and at school and stuff.'

Micheál shook his head. It was his own fault. He was the one who broke up their group. Or his mother did. Or the land did, those cursed cliffs. He didn't know anymore.

'It's alright,' he said.

'I mean, I'm guessing you have your own shite going on at home.'

'Yeah.'

Tuan's face was lost in smoke for a moment. 'You should get the fuck away from there as quickly as possible, lad.'

'That's the plan,' Micheál said. The Leaving Cert was only a year away. His mother wanted him to stay close. He could do a course in the IT in Tralee and commute from home, she'd said. But he was looking further afield. Cork, Limerick, Galway, maybe even Dublin. As soon as he got his place in university, he'd be away. Free.

He nudged Tuan. Maybe he would take a cigarette after all.

26

He wakes to the weight of Sammy spread across his shins at the bottom of the bed. He always searches him out during storms like this, when it's difficult to tell apart the fierce sounds of sea and sky.

His phone on the bedside table reads 03.47 a.m. Two hours, thereabouts. More than he's managed the last couple of nights. He's had bouts like this before and they always pass. It's not like he ever sleeps well here, anyway; a part of him always switched on. This is not so different.

Camomile tea – he'd bought some on his most recent excursion to Brenda's. No sign of Aengus this time, though he'd heard the TV on upstairs, canned laughter. Maybe the tea would get him an extra hour or two of sleep. With care, he slips his legs from under Sammy, rises out of bed and makes for the kitchen, dressing gown hanging on him, untied.

He flicks the switch in the kitchen, is relieved to see light – even if it means squinting for a moment until his eyes adjust. Through the window, the moon flits in and out of view. Only December and this is already the eighth named storm of the season: Harry. The name of a chartered accountant. Yellow warning for rain across the entire country; amber wind warning for the west coast. He'd made sure to bring in the bins before it landed. Mid-afternoon, daylight already dimming, he'd watched seabirds fly inland ahead of the storm: mostly gannet, seagulls, some cormorant. Though it was hard to identify great skua at a distance, he thought he spotted a flock of them at one point: dark, gull-like birds, with prominent white flashes in the outer wing. Whatever they were, he hopes they found a safe spot to see out the storm.

Kettle boiled, he fills his cup three quarters full, adds the tea bag, then tops up from the cold tap. The camomile had been Áine's suggestion the last time this happened, after Nadine. It hadn't worked then, but maybe it would now.

Áine had called again today, this time to give him one final chance to accept her invite to Christmas dinner. He said thanks but no thanks, as he did every year. There had been no word on her feelers feeling anything yet, and he had no intention of asking. The sudden sounds of childish argument in the background, a feral scream, feet stomping upstairs. Sensing she was about to end the conversation, he said, 'I see Aengus Dillane is back.'

'He is, alright.'

'How did that come about?'

'Ah, you know how they are. They've always been on and off like this; now they're just on again.'

'Even after the way he treated her the last time?'

'Well, look, it's not like any of us are experts when it comes to relationships, are we?'

He grimaced. 'Fair enough.'

'But you know with them it'll likely be off again by the New Year.'

'Yeah, could be.'

Micheál sips his tea as the wind shifts, slapping rain against the east-facing window. He takes another sip, though that feeling he gets when he knows that sleep is beyond him has settled on him now. Maybe 'feeling' is the wrong word; it's more like a frequency, and once it comes he knows that there will be no tuning back into sleep.

Another strong gust and the light flickers; any moment now and it will go out.

XXVII

His last night at home, his mother said little. She fretted about in the kitchen, glancing out the window even more frequently than usual. His sisters hid away in their bedrooms. After packing, Micheál walked down the hallway and knocked on Áine's door. The Smiths groaned away on the other side. She'd borrowed the cassette from him a week earlier, and he realised in that moment that he wouldn't be getting it back. He knocked again.

'What?' Áine shouted.

'Can I come in?'

No response. After a few seconds, Micheál opened the door. Inside, the room was its usual spotless self, as she sat on top of her already-made bed, posters of Sinéad O'Connor and The Cranberries behind her and a notebook on her lap. She held one of those multi-colour, retractable pens in her hand, the red nib pressed down.

He sat on the windowsill. 'Writing about me, are you?'

'You really do think you're the centre of the universe, don't you?' she said, her gaze still stuck in her notebook.

Micheál leaned forward, readied himself to say what he'd come to say. 'Look, Áine, if she asks you to help her, don't, okay? Just don't.'

'Help her with what?' she asked.

'You know what. And don't let her rope in Saoirse either. Let her keep on doing it herself, if she wants. But ye need to stay clear of it, okay? Just stand up to her and say no.'

She finally looked at him. 'Like you did?'

'Áine, come on.'

'We'll be fine, Mick. Don't worry about us. I'll make sure of it.'

She turned back to her notebook, red ink scratching across the page.

28

The worst part of insomnia is the boredom. Laid out in bed for hours, waiting for the oblivion of sleep. He tries to keep his mind clear, but this stretched-out time allows him too much opportunity to think. Tonight it is Nadine who clouds his head.

Conceding defeat, he sits up and grabs his laptop from the bedside table. It has been years since he's done this, but he feels compelled, now, in the dark. The glare from the screen makes him squint; he turns down the brightness and types into the search engine. He deleted his page shortly after Nadine left, but knows that one or two clicks will restore it. He does this without thinking. Jesus, he looks young in his profile; he forgets how baby-faced he appears without the beard – though that is unlikely to still be the case. He searches for Nadine's page. Open to friends only, he still sees her profile picture: her smiling in a silk-looking red sleeveless dress, the type she'd wear to a wedding. Her hair is shorter now and a lighter shade than he remembers. It is a punch to the heart, seeing her life unfolding in parallel to his own. He sometimes forgets that she is still out there, existing.

He clicks on to June's page. Nadine's best friend since primary school, she must have forgotten to unfriend him, or maybe he'd deleted his account before she had the chance. He scrolls down, soon finds a dozen photos marked 'Engagement Party – Nadine & Alan xxx'. He doesn't recognise most of the people in the photos. In one picture, Nadine stands beside a tall, fit-looking man, a tuft of chest hair visible with the top two buttons of his azure, tight-fitting shirt undone. His arm is draped around her, a smug-seeming smile cut through designer stubble. He is tagged in the photo: Alan O'Driscoll.

He clicks on to Alan's page, which is set to public. The profile picture is of him and Nadine somewhere foreign. A Mediterranean setting, he'd guess. Education: Blackrock College, Trinity. Works at Mulcahy & Francis Associates. His cover photo is of the Leinster rugby emblem. Nadine's father wouldn't be impressed with that, he thinks. No chance he'd bring a Leinster fan to Thomond.

He knows he should stop; this isn't healthy. It certainly won't help him sleep. But he keeps scrolling.

XXIX

'Shots?'

The offer went up from Jamie. That afternoon, he'd earned the nickname 'Coxie', after coxing the novice eight in their first regatta. They'd finished last, but were determined not to let that dampen their night out. Micheál added a 'Go on, so' to the affirmative noises in the corner booth in Reidy's, an Old Eriny-type pub, all turf fires, black-and-white photos of morose-looking Gaels against empty fields, that had some sort of connection to the rowing club. The tray of shots arrived almost immediately, the liqueur water-clear but with thin, gold flakes floating in them.

'What is it?' Ronan asked, shoulders on him like a wrestler. An advocate of creatine and microwaving entire chickens for lunch, he had been an obvious choice for the centre of the boat for the race, where all the power was, as it'd been explained to Micheál. He had been surprised to be deemed 'enough of a lump', by Tom Flannery, the novice coach, to find himself in the centre too.

'Goldschläger,' Jamie said.

Darren, by far the drunkest at the table, his too-tight T-shirt reading 'Talent Spotter', held his shot glass aloft. 'See the flecks, they're actual gold. The whole thing with them, right, is that they make tiny little cuts in your throat as it goes down, so the alcohol gets into your bloodstream and you get drunk faster.'

'Bullshit,' Ronan said. 'No chance that's true.'

'I'm telling you, it is,' Darren said.

'Whoever told you that is taking the piss,' Ronan insisted.

'Take it up with your mother, so, coz she told me last night.'

A pantomime 'Oooooh' from the table. Micheál joined the laughter. He'd heard so many of these conversations from a distance in school; it felt good to be on the inside of one. This was what he'd been imagining for himself since that conversation years earlier, he and his mother sitting before the exposed heart of Christ. A group of friends. Nights out. A laugh. The possibility of a deep night's sleep away from the cliffs. This was what Limerick had been for him so far, an exhalation of sorts. The rowing club, which he'd joined by chance during orientation week after being handed a flyer, was at the heart of it.

'Alright, calm down,' Jamie urged Darren.

Each of them took a shot glass, raised it. 'To last place,' Jamie said. 'Last place,' the rest echoed. Micheál felt the shot burn on its way down, imagined countless tiny nicks along his oesophagus, gold in his blood.

They began replaying the race: their decent start in choppy waters, that crosswind; still, they had put in an admirable effort, until Micheál's oar had snagged in the water, swinging round, nearly hitting him in the head and pulling him from the boat. Ronan, in the seat behind, had been forced to grab him to stop him falling overboard.

'You were lucky you didn't get knocked out,' Ronan said.

Micheál felt all eyes turn to him. 'I know, I know,' he replied, sensing himself redden. Leaving the lake afterwards, all eight lifting the boat into the air, he expected to be scorned or exiled. Instead, there had just been banter, the odd dig. No one was taking it too seriously. They were novices, after all.

'How will he make it up to us?' Darren pondered.

'Shots?' Micheál ventured.

'Shots!' they all cheered.

En route to the bar, he saw some of the more established rowers from the club huddled together near the exit. Including Nadine. He had first seen her at the boathouse along the Shannon on a crisp Saturday morning before his first session on the river. Across the hall, she powered away, red-faced, on an erg machine, watery light from outside catching in her blondish-brown ponytail. As Flannery tried to teach him and his fellow novices basic technical skills – 'Many people think you need to pull with the arms, but you should be pushing off with the legs; that's where the real power lies' – his gaze kept returning to her, astride the erg. He couldn't explain why, but he sensed that her technique was perfect.

They'd shared the odd nod or greeting since, but nothing close to an actual conversation. Hovering at the bar, he noticed that she was set to leave. He felt tipsy enough to say something, but not too drunk that what he said would be guaranteed gibberish, so he moved towards her, caught her eye.

'Congrats on the win,' he said, hoping she thought the blush in his cheeks was from the drink.

She smiled. 'Right, thanks – Micheál, isn't it?'

'That's me,' he said, trying to suppress a grin.

'How'd your race go?' she asked.

'Ah, not great; we came last. Mainly because I caught a crab,' he said, slipped in the rowing term he'd learned from the others earlier.

'We've all done that.' She offered a sympathetic grimace. 'But it was the first race for most of ye, right? It'll get easier, don't worry.'

'I hope so; I nearly fell out of the boat. I mean, it wasn't so much a crab as a whale.'

She laughed.

He nodded towards the coat in the crook of her arm. 'You're leaving, are you?'

'Yeah, have an early lecture in the morning, and anyway I don't drink much once the race season starts.'

'That's commitment,' he said.

She shrugged. 'I suppose.'

The only thing Micheál had committed to, of late, was leaving behind Kerry Head. He'd promised Áine and Saoirse that he would travel home as often as he could, but he kept finding reasons to stay away. Assignments. Exams. His two part-time jobs – one in a run-down café off O'Connell Street, the other in Bradley's, a newsagent's in the Johnsgate section of the city. Nights out like this. It was as though his years as an outcast in secondary school had given him pent-up energy for socialising. Since arriving at Mary Immaculate College, he'd gone to class parties, joined the English Lit Society, the Film Society, the Hill Walkers Club, the rowing. Nearly three months into college life, he'd yet to return home.

'Can I walk you to your taxi?' he asked.

She hesitated, then smiled a smile that contained layers he couldn't quite reach. 'Sure,' she said.

Micheál rushed back to his table, grabbed his coat and handed Ronan thirty quid. 'Buy the next round with that; I'll be back in a few minutes.'

He frowned. 'Where are you going?'

'Text me if ye move on.'

Outside, they wandered down O'Connell Street past late-night revellers. When they reached the taxi rank it was empty, so they kept walking. Micheál watched as a young man, likely a fellow student, vomited beside a bike rack down one of the many side streets that he couldn't yet name, the topography of the inner city still only half-known to him.

A taxi approached and Micheál held his hand aloft.

'The light is off,' Nadine pointed out.

'Worth a try.'

The taxi drove by, though no passengers seemed to be inside.

'Maybe he's finished for the night?' she said.

'Sick of all us drunken youths.'

'Speak for yourself.'

She pointed at one of the side streets and they turned down it, the river ahead, black mostly, though the edges were frayed amber by street light. 'Sometimes down here you can catch a taxi coming back from a fare,' she explained.

'Do you have far to go?' he asked.

'Castletroy.'

He shrugged.

'It's out near the UL campus, which is handy for lectures and all that. Turns out that studying physiotherapy is fairly full on.'

'Oh, that's cool – that you're close to campus, I mean. Not the heavy workload.'

'Well, it also means still living with my parents.'

Micheál grunted. 'Ouch; must be tough.'

'Ah, it's not too bad. We get on well enough, and they have no problem with me staying over at friends' some nights, if I'm out.'

'What's that like?'

'What?'

'Getting on well with your family?'

She turned to look at him properly for the first time. He kept his eyes on the street and then stepped forward, arm out, when he saw another taxi, its light on this time. The taxi drove by without slowing. A part of Micheál thrilled at its passing.

'Do you have a big family?' she asked.

'Just my mam and two sisters. You?'

'I'm an only child.'

'That must be nice,' he said.

She shrugged. 'So everyone with siblings says to me,

anyway. But, like, I've never known it to be any different, you know? It's funny, though – when I was little I was certain that the term was "lonely child". It made more sense to me, I guess?' She shrugged and they both laughed.

Another taxi appeared on the bridge, light ablaze. Hand raised to neon sky. Again, it sped by. 'Should we just start walking in the direction of Castletroy?' he suggested.

'It's like an hour's walk.'

'We're bound to hail a taxi on the way. I can't look that shady.'

She raised an eyebrow.

'Hey.'

'Joking, joking.' She pointed eastward along the river. 'Okay, we should go this way.'

They followed what seemed to be the same road – though there were many roundabouts – out of the city centre, the restaurants, bars and tall Georgian buildings replaced with apartment blocks, takeaways, hairdressers, bookies, rows of old, squat houses. Once they passed a hospital, a car parked askew by the entrance to the A&E. They saw no taxis on the road.

'So the rowing,' he said, eager to keep talking. To discover more about her.

'Yeah?'

'Are you as good as they say? It sounds like you're the star of the club, the way they talk about you. In fact, I'm surprised you're even willing to talk to such a lowly novice like me.'

'I'm alright, like. I mean, I'd want to be for the amount of time I put into it.'

'Oh yeah?'

'Yeah, like I'd be on the water every day, pretty much; there's the gym work, the hill runs twice a week, the erg work. You need to give it everything, really, if you want to be any good at it. Of course, that doesn't leave much time for anything else.'

'Sounds like it, alright.'

Another roundabout. Micheál's heels, in new black shoes bought for ten quid in Dunnes Stores two weeks earlier, were beginning to cut, but he forced the discomfort aside, continued walking.

'Do you know Juniper?' she asked.

'The band?'

'Yeah. I'm going to see them next week in Riordan's with a group from the club.'

'That's cool. I didn't know they were playing. I love them. I still can't believe Damien Rice was stupid enough to leave the group; they're going to be huge.'

'I know, right?' She scratched at her eyebrow, looked not so much at him as slightly over his eyeline, as if he had something in his hair. 'Anyway, there are a few tickets left, I think, if you wanted to come along.'

He felt himself blush, knew he couldn't blame alcohol this time. 'I'd like that, yeah. I mean, that'd be cool.'

Ahead, a taxi appeared. Light on.

Neither raised a hand as it approached, drove past.

30

On his return from the fort, Micheál sees Spillane in his field, hands on hips, staring out across the bay. The man must be in his seventies, but he still looks solid, little different now than when Micheál first saw him over three decades ago. Funny how working the land seems to wear down some, while others, if anything, grow sturdier, more substantial, as if drawing strength from the very earth on which they toil.

He salutes. 'Happy Christmas.'

Spillane waves back. 'And to you.'

As he climbs towards the bungalow, Micheál thinks of the day ahead. He will cook himself a fine meal once inside; he even bought a turkey for the day that was in it. Leftovers will do him for the week, and he can feed Sammy the scraps. He also has a present for the dog: a raw beef bone picked up yesterday from Danny Glavin, the butcher in the village. Then there will be a video call from Áine and her lot: a twenty-to-thirty-minute check-in where Áine talks him through her hectic morning, Brian gives a polite wave and a 'You're well, Mick?' before returning to the TV, and Ryan and Damien breathlessly tell him what Santa brought and are prompted into thanking him for the presents he sent. This call has become a tradition in recent years, and though he feels awkward on video – his gaze drawn to his fun-house-mirror face in the corner of the screen – it will be pleasant to see them, to have other voices fill the bungalow for a time.

At the house, he sits on the windowsill, looks across the bay. It is a clear day, crisp, the peninsula opposite shades of deep blue and heather-brown. Almost directly south, on the far peninsula, is the site of another Christmas tradition, one that marked every year of his childhood. After early Mass, his mother would drive the four of them to the graveyard in Tralee, lay wreaths at the graves of his grandparents, his father. Rather than return home, she then drove through town, past the windmill at Blennerville and out the Dingle peninsula. Beyond Camp, they climbed into the mountains, the bay stretching out beneath them, Micheál and his sisters pointing at the lighthouse by Fenit, the outstretched arm of the Maharees, and Kerry Head in the distance. Each of them taking turns to lie, say they could see the white flare of their house.

High in the mountains, a valley now below them – a patchwork of fields, speckling of houses and woodland – his mother indicated, took a narrow green-spined road down into the valley. This was Gleann na nGealt. Valley of the Mad. His mother would tell them stories of the place: how for hundreds of years people – the sick, the sad, and those called mad – came or were brought there to drink from a well within the valley. Its water was said to have restorative powers, would quell the turmoil within, bring peace, for a time. Growing up, Micheál was never sure whether to believe his mother, but some of the local history books he's been reading have confirmed that most of what she told them about the valley is true. One such book, *The Ancient and Present State of the County of Kerry*, written by a historian called Charles Smith in 1756, recounted the 'fable' of the well, which drew 'all the mad folks of the kingdom' seeking its healing effects. If it was so widely known in Smith's day, people must have been coming to the valley for a long time before that.

Micheál's mother saw a link between this place and theirs. How families in the valley, generations of them, helped the distressed visitors who pilgrimaged to that remote spot. Led them to the well, took them in and cared for them – for weeks or even months in some cases. 'We are tied into the same tradition,' she said, though Micheál wondered if their land was, in fact, a counterpoint to the valley: the black spot to its white.

Once parked near the entrance, Micheál's mother made each child carry two plastic bottles to the well. Micheál and Áine, like their mother, lugged the five-litre plastic-handled Ballygowan bottles; Saoirse was given two-litre bottles to carry under her arms. A wooden sign had been placed in the roadside ditch: Tobar Na nGealt. Well of the Mad. After an opening in the ditch, they walked through undergrowth to what was, in reality, not so much a well as a spring, from which a small stream flowed. What Micheál remembers most are the offerings that hung from branches above the spring and along the stream: bracelets, rosaries, strips of clothing. Little ornaments poked out from among the watercress. An uneasiness always gripped him when there; he would fill the bottles in a rush, eager to get away.

His mother often offered the visitors this water, said it would help. Told them the story of the valley. Some accepted, others declined. Micheál sometimes saw her sneak it into their drinks anyway. He wonders if she did this to him and his sisters. He wouldn't put it past her. She drank a shot glass of it every morning with her breakfast.

Micheál found an article about the valley online last year.

It included the details of a scientific testing of the spring water. And it turns out that they did find something of note: the water contains significantly higher than usual traces of lithium. The scientist quoted in the article was sceptical as to whether this raised amount would have any therapeutic value – though he didn't entirely discount it, and neither could he rule out that the levels of lithium may have been higher in decades and centuries past. He concluded by saying that maybe it was something about the place, the belief people had in it. That's what brought all those people such solace.

Sammy whines, waiting by the door. He is hungry now.

'Were you always this demanding?' Micheál asks, turning away from the bay. A quick look at the time on his phone. Shit. Better get started on the dinner if he wants to have eaten before Áine calls.

XXXI

Nadine drove with an unusual restraint, never straying over the limit on the motorway out of the city, indicating not once but twice at the roundabout into Adare, stopping at a traffic light in Newcastle West though it only shone amber. Normally, she drove like she rowed: all foot-down speed, as if every journey were a race. But then this wasn't the only difference in her that Sunday afternoon. Normal attire for Nadine was tracksuit pants, a T-shirt, the rowing club or UL hoodie if cold. Hair ponytailed, no make-up. Now, she looked like she was going to Mass, or an interview.

'Are they alright, do you think?' she asked, gesturing to the box of Milk Tray wrapped in a Dunnes plastic bag on the back seat.

'They are, yeah. The girls will love them, anyway, and I'm sure Mam will sneak one or two.'

Ahead, on either side of the road, a sign read: welcome to the kingdom of kerry.

Nadine chuckled. 'Welcome to the sticks is more like it.'

'Hey.'

'Scenic sticks, to be fair.'

Near the turn-off for Crag Cave, he noticed her index finger tap repeatedly against the top of the steering wheel.

He put a hand on her thigh. 'It'll be fine, Nad; they're going to love you.'

This visit was long overdue. Nadine often asked about his family and when she would get to meet them. He had only given her the bare bones of his past. He intimated that his relationship with his mother was strained, though he did not elaborate, and Nadine had mostly refrained from pressing. Still, after their one-year anniversary the previous week, and another mention by Nadine, he could hold off no longer. He rang home, let his mother know they were coming.

'So I'm finally getting to meet the reason why you never come home?'

'She's not the reason. You know that.'

The delay in introducing Nadine to his family particularly jarred given the amount of time he spent with hers. Since she lived at home, he met them early on in the relationship. Her father owned a car dealership and always – even around the house – wore suit trousers, a shirt and tie. His idea of casual seemed to be loosening the tie and unbuttoning the top button, two at most. Despite this, he was a warm man, who tried to make Micheál feel comfortable when he visited. He often wanted to talk about football, likely because Micheál was from Kerry. He seemed unable to comprehend that he'd grown up in a hurling stronghold. 'But do Kerry even have a hurling team?' he asked more than once. Nadine's mother was a short, broad-shouldered woman with cropped brown hair. An accountant, she had played inter-county football for Limerick back in the early eighties. One of her front teeth was a fake, knocked out by Nora Fitzgerald, a Kerry midfielder. 'But I won't hold that against you.'

Micheál was surprised by how easy-going Nadine's parents were; they even had no issue with him staying the night in her bedroom. So he found himself staying at the Fordes' a lot. And he began to see the closeness of their dynamic, centred around a shared love of sport. Most of their conversations revolved around it. Micheál found himself following more sports, keeping on top of news and results, keen to find a way into their daily rhythms: 'Did you hear Keane might be out for the game?' 'No, what happened?' 'Rumour is that he strained his calf.' Once, when Nadine had training and couldn't go to a rugby game, her father offered her ticket to Micheál. Rugby was one of his sporting blind spots, but he swotted up, and by the time of the game knew enough to follow the action. Soon he was regularly going with Nadine's father to Thomond Park, and even travelled up to Lansdowne Road a couple of times. So, really, a visit to Kerry Head was long overdue.

As they drove through Ballyheigue, he noticed construction

going on in the field behind Brenda's: the skeletal frames of semi-detached houses; a digger with its arm half-raised, the bucket curled inwards, giving the machine a hunched and mournful appearance. A new estate? Looked like the Celtic Tiger had finally reached the village. Out the headland, his stomach tumbled into such a state that he felt unsure if he'd be able for lunch. Nadine wore an expression that he recognised from before her races: focused, determined, eager to do her best.

When they parked outside the house, she looked at him, open-mouthed: 'You didn't tell me you lived inside a fucking Bord Fáilte advert? It's incredible.' He felt an anger build in him even before he stepped out of the car. A part of it was directed towards Nadine, making him come back here when it was the last place he wanted to be; part towards his mother, for the pained looks he knew she would fling his way throughout the afternoon. And part was a general anger towards the universe for making what should have been a good day something that would instead likely be awkward, frustrating and maybe even ruinous. What if his mother or sisters said something about the visitors? What if one actually showed up during the lunch? He hadn't found the right time to tell Nadine yet. Couldn't bear the thought of scaring her away, of jeopardising the new life that he'd built for himself in Limerick.

Áine opened the door just as he was about to knock. 'Welcome, welcome,' she said, smiling, though there was no hug, no handshake offered to Nadine. Micheál hadn't noticed before how the first thing you saw when the door opened was Jesus with his lightbulb heart.

'Come in.'

The smell of gravy and the chicken roasting in the oven hit him once inside. The table had been set with their best crockery. Micheál's gaze fell on the flashlight stationed on the counter by the door, a wool hat and balled-up gloves beside it. He hoped Nadine wouldn't notice them, that if she did, she would not wonder why they were arranged so carefully in that spot. He thought for a moment. Nightwalking, he could say, if she asked. Yes. His mother liked to walk the road at night, brought the flashlight with her so she was seen by approaching cars.

Micheál's mother stood by the cooker, in her bright bird-patterned apron, wooden spoon in hand. She walked over, gave Nadine a hug. 'It's lovely to finally meet you,' she said.

Nadine handed her the box of Milk Tray. 'Thanks for having me,' she said.

'It's no trouble; Micheál should have brought you down far sooner than this.'

Micheál began, 'Well, the course load, and with the rowing and my part-time job on the weekends . . .'

'He's always saying how much he misses home,' Nadine lied. He hoped his own expression hid his surprise.

'Does he now?' his mother said, glancing at him. 'Well, he's missed here too.'

Micheál fixed his gaze out the sink window.

'Sorry, but where's the bathroom?' Nadine asked.

Micheál felt a surge of panic, wanted to say: *Hold it, you can hold it*, but Áine directed her to the second door on the right down the hallway and in a moment Nadine and the protection her presence offered was gone. He could see both his mother and Áine winding up. To forestall them, he blurted: 'Where's Saoirse?'

'She's over at Stephanie's,' his mother said, a hesitancy in her voice. 'They're working on some project for school together and the deadline's tomorrow.'

Micheál sensed a lie in this, and when he glanced at Áine her gaze fell to the floor. Maybe Saoirse refused to see him, had decided to avoid him in the same way that he avoided this place, his family.

'Stephanie?' he asked.

Áine glowered. 'Her best friend. Jesus, Mick.'

Further discussion was stalled by a flush, a faucet running. Nadine appeared out of the bathroom, walked down the hallway towards them. It touched on the surreal to see her in the narrow, linoleum-covered hallway. She seemed too big for such a space. Big was the wrong word, he knew, but it was something along those lines.

'Right, all of you sit down there. The dinner is ready,' his mother announced.

Nadine was the only one of them to waver. 'Can I help with anything?' she asked.

'No, no, just sit yourself down there.'

The lunch was surprisingly low-key and pleasant. He had expected his mother to be cold towards Nadine after what she'd said on the phone, but she remained welcoming and warm, drawing Nadine out of herself with questions and even telling stories about Micheál as a child: the time he tried to ride a neighbour's Labrador, the time he ate three of his father's cigarettes, the time he knocked out his front two baby teeth climbing on to the TV – 'I think he was trying to climb into it, really; he wanted to play with Big Bird and Elmo.' Nadine and Áine talked about Anne Rice, *Dawson's Creek*, *Buffy the Vampire Slayer*. At one point, Nadine asked her about her upcoming Leaving Cert exams.

'You all set for them?'

Áine shrugged. 'I think so; I've definitely put a lot of study time in.'

'Cool. And what about after? Do you know what course you want to do? Which college?'

Áine looked at Micheál as she spoke. 'No, I'm actually going to hold off on college for a bit, stay a year or two out here. Think about what it is I really want to do.'

Micheál met Áine's pointed gaze. It confirmed what he'd suspected: her decision to delay leaving here had nothing to do with figuring out what she wanted to do. She would do what he had failed to do. Stay behind, not allow Saoirse to be burdened with the visitors in the way that she had been, wait for her younger sister to finish school and then leave this place together.

'You're sure about this?' he asked.

'I am.'

His mother interrupted: 'Anyone for more gravy?'

Afterwards, as they drove back to Limerick, Nadine said that his mother and sister seemed lovely; if anything, it was Micheál who had been awkward and cold. 'You hardly said anything. And were you expecting someone to show up or what?' she asked.

'No, why?'

'You kept looking out the window.'

It was only when they arrived back at Nadine's house that evening that he felt he could breathe again.

32

Micheál has almost found sleep when his phone rattles atop the bedside table, a weak projection of electronic light plastering the ceiling. He rolls over, reads the screen as the wind hurls abuse against the window.

Áine. He looks at the time on the top right-hand corner of the screen: 00.13. She must be ringing to wish him a happy New Year. Pleased with him now that he's playing ball. Even if she knows that he has half a mind to fling the ball over the cliffs. He lets the phone ring out, the ceiling return to darkness. He is in no mood to talk to her, but he also knows that if he wakes more, he'll end up online again, searching out Nadine. That needs to stop. All that is as much ancient history as the fort up the road. Still, for a long time after the ringing ends, he has to fight the urge to reach for the phone, search out her profile.

He turns away from the bedside table, curls foetal. Focus on your breathing. In, out; in, out.

Another wind-screech. The sensor light clicks on.

He is out of bed in a moment, squinting out the window. He sees nothing. Sometimes a strong wind can do that, trick the sensor, turn the wind into something solid, sentient. But he knows he has to venture into the elements anyway.

The wind blows back the hood of his mac as soon as he

steps outside, his hair drenched in the time it takes to raise it back in place. A glance towards the gate. Closed. A dart and scan of the flashlight up the field towards the cliffs. Nothing. But an odd sense remains, lying close to goose-bumped skin. It was not the wind that set off the light. The air feels charged in a way that it only does when someone else is present.

He leans into the wind and rain, climbs towards the cliff. The flashlight falls on long grass, protruding rocks near the cliffs. No visitor. He slips, right knee and hand falling to wet earth. Fuck sake, what was he doing? No one is here, he tells himself; no one but the echoes of those who have come before.

He turns back towards the house, resigned, and it is in this moment that the charge in the air takes shape: a lighted flint of sky bolts down to Illauntannig, blazing the whole island to life; another, branching down, strikes the dark churn of water, and another follows: chasing along the clouds, searching out the faraway horizon.

Micheál watches all of this, soaked through, knee and palm muddied, as around him the whole world begins to thunder.

XXXIII

Nadine lay curled up on the furthest sliver of mattress from him, still in her going-out clothes: low-cut denim jeans and her 'dressy' top, as she called it, a black lace halterneck with a line of sparkling stones of some sort across the neckline. With every exhale, he heard the nose whistle she had as a result of a flailing oar at thirteen, deviating her septum. Still asleep. He had been awake for hours, turning the evening over in his mind. The fight in the smoking area of Reidy's, continued on the way to the nightclub, the taxi back to his place. One of Nadine's few nights able to let loose, with the rowing season finished, and he'd ruined it.

He manoeuvred to the side of the bed, feet finding grubby carpet, the chewed-on cap of a biro. Downstairs, he could hear Ronan chatting to the girl he'd brought home, a caterpillar-browed dentistry student from Tipperary called Denise. Micheál and three of the lads from the novice team had gone in on the house together at the start of the previous year, and had decided to remain in the jaundice-coloured semi-detached for Third Year, though only Ronan and he continued to row.

He noted the change in her breathing. A sort of taut stillness to her form when he turned around. 'Can I get you something?' he ventured. 'Tea?'

She sat up, the stones across her neck catching in the morning sun, casting a sharp light. Smudged mascara made warpaint of her under-eyes. She let out a deep, weary sigh. 'We can't keep having the same fight, Mick.'

'I know.'

'I mean, Louise came over to me at one point and was, like, why do you guys always fight when you're drunk, and I couldn't honestly tell her why.'

'Lucky you don't drink much, then, right?' he tried to joke. Her expression told him that it failed to land.

He flicked the biro cap aside with his foot, stood. 'I'll get us some water.'

Downstairs, the kitchen was now empty. Ronan and the dentist-to-be had retreated to his bedroom. He took two pint glasses from the press, both lifted from Reidy's to replace ones they had broken. He ran the water until it turned cold. It had all been fine till Gerard Devine swanned in. The other star junior rower of the club, along with Nadine. And didn't he fucking know it. Lording it about the place. And, as usual, he made a beeline straight for Nadine. 'Pint, Nads?' Grin flashed, eyes never straying from her, despite Micheál standing right beside her. 'No thanks,' she said. A shrug from Devine. 'Next time, then.'

He tried not to let it get to him, the flagrancy of his want, but with each drink it built in him. He forgot exactly how it came out, but he knew he made some remark, about inviting it, encouraging him – as if that gom ever needed any encouragement – and soon they were at it, again. And, once riled, Nadine fired back: at his closed-offness, whatever dark shit he had going on inside him that he didn't trust her enough to let her in on – 'It's not that,' he said; 'Then tell me, for fuck sake' – his desire to spend so much time at her house, with her parents: 'They're my fucking parents, stop trying to reverse adopt them, alright!'

He mouthed a curse as he turned off the tap. Jesus, but the drink made it all so messy. He carried the glasses upstairs, spilling some on his hands, the stairs' wine-red carpet. He heard giggling from Ronan's room and grimaced. In his bedroom, Nadine had propped herself up, the pillow a cushion for her lower back against the headrest. The *Before Sunrise* poster on the wall mocked him, them, amid the ruins of the night before. He handed her the water, sat at the end of the bed. 'There you go now,' he said, just to say something.

'Thanks.'

He sipped at the water, let it rest between his thighs, the cool dampness felt through his shorts.

'We can't keep fighting about the same stuff,' she repeated.

'I know, but . . .'

'What?'

'Nothing.'

'What?'

He knew he should restrain himself, that what he wanted to say was stupid, pathetic, insecure. But the words inside him had the texture and propulsion of vomit; he felt an inability to keep it all down. 'I mean, you know he wants to fuck you, right?'

'Oh my God, Mick.'

'What?'

'Even if he does want to fuck me, it doesn't matter; all that matters is who I want to fuck. Do you understand?'

He blushed. 'I do, yeah. I know.'

'Do you?'

'I know, yeah. I'm sorry.'

'And that's you, dipshit. I mean, not right now – I'm hung-over and still pissed with you. But usually, when you're not acting like a drunken, jealous dick, I generally like the idea of fucking you.'

'Good to know.'

She reached over, punched him in the shoulder, not lightly. 'Not Gerard Devine, right?'

'Right.'

'I imagine he can only ever cum while masturbating furiously into a mirror, anyway. Or to photos of himself in a one-piece.'

Micheál snorted. 'Sounds about right.'

She rubbed her head, as if only now feeling the hangover. 'Any Dioralyte or Lucozade or something downstairs?'

He stood. 'I'll check.'

'Mick.'

He stopped near the door, turned. 'Yeah?'

She focused her gaze on her upturned hands, picking at a callus beneath her middle finger. 'You'll get on top of this, won't you? I want to have a fun night out with you; I don't want to keep worrying that we'll explode whenever we're out, you know. You really do have to get on top of this, like.'

'I know. I'm sorry; it won't happen again,' he promised.

'Yeah?'

'Yeah.'

Something in the way she turned her gaze away from him at the end of that conversation, towards her upturned palm, the rough skin, let him know that this was how he could lose her. So he found a way to control things, and maybe even convinced himself for a time that he had bested it. Though he wonders now if he ever did lose those feelings – *You're not good enough for her; as soon as she knows the real you, what you really come from, what you've done, she'll leave you for someone better* – if, instead of spewing them out drunkenly, they only pooled inside him, curdling in his gut, bile on bile.

He is an odd sight in his pin-striped suit and grey wellies. Gary Dwyer, he'd introduced himself on arriving. No relation to the neighbours; not that he knew of, anyway. Now he stands in the field, digital camera raised, taking a slew of photos, as if he wants to capture every possible angle of the land.

'He looks about twelve,' Micheál says.

Áine grunts. 'The suit only makes him seem younger, if anything. It's like he's playing at being an adult. The wellies don't help, I suppose.'

'You'd think Halloran would come out himself – I would have thought he'd want to see the land before trying to buy it.'

'He's a busy man, Mick. Busy people delegate.'

'Suppose.'

Áine's feelers had felt out Jim Halloran, a developer based in Tralee, surprisingly fast. Even suspiciously fast. He suspects that she had already approached Halloran prior to getting his approval. Not that he can prove it, and anyway there is no point in bringing it up. It's done now. And just because there is interest doesn't mean he has to agree to sell.

'I had my check-up yesterday, by the way. Start of every year. Got the all-clear. When was your last one?' she asks.

Since their mother's death, Áine has taken on the responsibility of plaguing him – and he assumes Saoirse – to get an annual check-up. To ensure none of them has inherited their father's cardiac fragility. If caught early, it can be managed, his mother told them; it's only if the condition is allowed to fester that real damage can be done.

'It's grand, I got it checked just before Christmas,' he lies. He hasn't been to a doctor since Nadine left.

Áine nods, seeming to believe him.

Gary has now moved closer to the cliffs. Though he knows there is nothing to worry about, Micheál still tenses. Habit, he supposes. He looks at Áine, whose attention has shifted to Sammy, laid out at her feet, looking to have his belly rubbed.

'So you think there's definitely a strong interest?' he asks.

'Seems to be. Gary was telling me on the way out how Halloran is certain that – what did he call them, "stay-cations"? – are the way forward. He went on about how the future of tourism is national, not international. And they feel our spot of land is perfect for a hotel. Whatever else you can say about this place, you can't knock the view.'

Micheál frowns. 'No, you can't. But surely he'd need planning permission and all that nonsense for something like that. Local approval.'

'He doesn't seem to think it'll be a problem.'

'No, I suppose it wouldn't be for someone like him.'

Áine continues to rub Sammy, pats his flank. 'We've lucked out here, Mick; I don't think we'll ever get a better chance than this to offload the place.'

He squints towards Gary, camera now aimed back at Áine and him, the house. He looks like a terrible spy, snapping away out in the open. 'Sure. I know.'

XXXV

Micheál was correcting homework on the bruised-blue couch in the apartment when he got a call from Nadine's number, though it was a man's voice that greeted him. 'Mick,' said Darren Casey, the rowing club's senior coach. 'Are you at your place?'

'Yeah.'

'Nadine said she left the car there. Can you drive it down to the clubhouse?'

'Why? What's wrong?' he asked, already standing.

It was one of those freak things, Casey said. Nadine was carrying the scull from the boathouse to the jetty, something she had done hundreds of times. The ground was wet underfoot from a recent shower, and, halfway down the slope, she slipped. 'The knee's banjaxed, Mick; you need to drive down to take her to A&E. I'd do it myself, but I cycled in today.'

'No, of course; I'll be right there.'

After hanging up, Micheál scoured the apartment for the car keys, checking the usual spots: the counter in the kitchen, still messed with the late lunch he'd made for himself after work; the ash stand in the hallway by the coat-rack; the pockets of his jacket, his raincoat; the faux-leather satchel he'd bought for his first teaching role. Nothing. The nightstand in the bedroom. No. Where else? 'Fuck,' he said, his heart thrilling now, thinking of Nadine, in pain, needing him. He checked the jacket he wore that morning again, patted his shirt, his pants. His arse pocket: a familiar jingle. *You fucking idiot.*

He raced down the stairs rather than wait for the lift to the basement car park. In the car the CD player blurted on. He switched it off. Right, focus. She needed him. Keys. Phone. Wallet. He drove out of the car park, turned right, towards the club. It was only a five-minute drive away. Proximity to the rowing club had been the main consideration in picking a place to rent, over a year ago now, after their graduation. He'd just been lucky that St Luke's, where he ended up getting a maternity-cover role, had also been nearby. Not that he minded; not really. Ronan had berated him for moving in with someone when still so young, but he had no regrets. Even if it did feel a little like playing house, playing at adult life.

Shit. The junction ahead was blocked up, horns blaring from different directions. A man walked past on the footpath wearing an odd-looking hat and Micheál flinched. After a few moments, he forced himself to look again. Not a homburg.

He remembered that he had to call Áine. As soon as he got his teaching job, Micheál had made sure to offer financial help to his sisters, both of whom were preparing to leave Kerry Head now that Saoirse was about to sit her Leaving Cert. Saoirse, who was planning to head to London, refused the offer outright. Áine had also declined the offer at the time. Last month, though, she got in touch, asking if he would be a guarantor for a student loan she was applying for ahead of starting Business Administration in the Institute of Technology in Cork. He hadn't heard anything from her since; he should check in, see if she needed anything else for the loan application, if she had heard anything.

His thoughts jumped back to Nadine, the injury. Please don't let it be too bad. After graduation, she had decided to give rowing her all for a few years, taking a part-time job at a leisure centre near Thomond and deferring a career in physiotherapy. 'I might even start my own clinic some day, but when the time's right, you know?' She spent every day now down at the boathouse. It made him realise that, from the beginning, he'd been attracted to her discipline, her single-mindedness. She'd found her passion, her vocation, sculpting her life around it. In contrast, he felt like he was adrift in his life, that the only real choice he had made – to train to become a teacher in Limerick – was one he was beginning to regret. Though at least it had led him to Nadine.

And her dedication was starting to pay off. That summer, her last at Under-23 level, she placed fourth in the national single sculls and fifth with her clubmate Nora Healy in the doubles. She'd then been selected as a sub for the Irish lightweight fours competing at that year's World Championship. The evening she heard, they'd gone out with her parents for a celebratory meal. A giddiness held all of them. Her father ordered champagne, though Nadine refused to drink any, not when she was in training. 'It's only a sub spot,' she said. Her father, cheeks puce with the drink, replied, 'Each step along the stepping stones deserves to be marked.' They all cheersed to that.

When he arrived at the club Nadine was sitting on a white plastic chair outside the boathouse, an ice pack wrapped in a floral tea towel placed atop her right knee. Micheál pulled the car up as close to her as he could. It was clear from her pinched, flared expression how much pain she was in. 'It was so stupid, so fucking stupid,' she kept saying as she was made to put an arm around both Micheál's and Darren's shoulders, and they helped her to the car. She spread across the back seat, so as not to bend her knee. 'I was already on the river in my head,' she said, as Micheál tied both seatbelts awkwardly across her.

Darren slapped the top of the car twice as they drove away. At the exit, Micheál stopped. St John's Hospital – that was the closest. He turned left, towards the inner city. A speckle of rain was falling, not yet heavy enough to turn on the wipers.

'Fuck it, anyway,' she sighed.

'I know, I know, Nad, but it'll be okay, you'll see. It probably feels worse than it actually is.'

He could see her shake her head in the rear-view mirror. 'It's the ACL, Mick; I know it is.'

'You don't know that.'

'Mick, I'm a qualified fucking physiotherapist; I think I know what type of injury it's likely to be.' She turned down the heat in her voice. 'This means nine months minimum out, more likely a year.'

'Yeah, but don't they have to scan the knee to confirm the injury? It could just be a strain instead of a tear, right?'

A drawn-out silence.

'Maybe.'

He could tell from the tightness of her voice that she was trying not to cry.

'So we won't panic just yet, okay? And whatever does happen, we'll get through it, okay?'

She sniffed, readjusted the ice pack on her knee. 'Okay.'

He approached a junction, stopped at the red light.

'Mick?'

He looked in the rear-view mirror. 'Yeah?'

She met his gaze. 'Thanks.'

'This is what I'm here for.'

He looked ahead again. Though the rain was strengthening, he still refused to turn on the wipers.

36

It's chance, really, that Micheál sees it coming.

He is lying on the Garfield mattress, watching three starlings flit and perch by the feeder, a sort of amicable yet frenzied waltz, when movement over Dwyer's land draws his gaze. Even with the naked eye, he can tell from the pointed wingspan against the clear, crisp sky and its sleek, almost insouciant flight that it is a raptor of some sort.

He lifts binoculars, trains his magnified sight towards the bird. After a few moments, he finds it, refocuses. That broad body and short, hooked bill mark it as a species of falcon, but is it a merlin or a peregrine? He's spotted merlin before but never a peregrine, though some were said to nest on the cliffs around Ballybunion. The yellow bill and white, finely barred underside is found on both species. The broader wings and the stronger moustache definitely suggest a peregrine. But it's hard to say for sure.

Above the boundary with Dwyer's land, the bird breaks, gaze fixed earthward. After a moment, it begins to climb. Seeing this, Micheál knows both that it is a peregrine falcon, and that he is about to witness something he has only seen on

YouTube, an act narrated by David Attenborough, for some BBC documentary. A peregrine 'stoop', where it descends at speeds of up to 200 miles an hour towards its prey, wings tucked in towards its body, killing it with the force of its impact, talons extended at the last moment.

Some poor field mouse is about to become lunch, he thinks, before a possibility tugs at him: doesn't a peregrine's diet usually consist of birds? His gaze swivels back to the starlings, four now, dancing about the feeder. He needs to bang against the window, warn them of the danger overhead, make them scatter. He takes his eyes from the scene outside, manoeuvres himself upright, but the few moments it costs him to reach the window is enough. When he looks out again, three starlings are fleeing to the south, and beneath the feeder, amid the long grass, the peregrine has its prey underfoot, hooked bill already dipped red.

XXXVII

Micheál hadn't expected the strand to be this busy. Walkers dotted the length of the wide sandy expanse, the tide well out, though on its way in. A team of some sort were training near the hotel, running in the heavy sand, sprinting up and down the dunes. When he'd imagined this evening, this walk, in recent weeks, he saw a romantic blaze of a horizon, but it was overcast, drizzly. Micheál and Nadine both wore wet-gear, hats; her hands were covered with slim cotton gloves, which could pose a problem later.

He glanced across at Nadine, saw a faint smile as she stared out to sea. The few days away had been a surprise for her: the fancy hotel, the cliff and beach walks, the spa package with seawater treatments, a massage, something to do with mud. He had hoped it would do her good to get away from the city, the river, for a time. And all the relaxing and spoiling appeared to be working; she looked easier in herself, the last few days.

The previous couple of years had been an ordeal – starting with the ACL injury, which a doctor had confirmed after a scan. Cartilage in the knee had been damaged, too, along with ligaments in her ankle. Those first few weeks and months, consigned to crutches, Nadine didn't know what to do with herself. Her days felt shapeless, she said, her life adrift. She spent most of her time on the couch, watching TV; he would join her in the evenings after doing corrections, his lesson plans. It was ten months before she got back in a boat: a calm, muggy day, with two swans floating nearby, a cygnet more white than grey trailing behind, its transition nearly complete. Afterwards, she was beaming: 'It felt sore, a bit stiff, but God it was good to get back on the water.' Soon, though, it became clear that things were not the same. The pain and stiffness in her knee remained, causing power and balance issues with her leg drive. Her times were a long way off her pre-injury level. And then her knee worsened. She had it scanned, consulted the club's physio. It was decided that she would have another operation. More crutches, more rehab. Still, upon her return, the stiffness remained. Her times refused to improve. Eventually, Darren Casey took her aside, said he was sorry but she had to face it – her dream of being an elite-level rower was over. She refused to leave the apartment for a month after that, hardly left the bed. It took her a long time to rise out of the pit of the injury. And even though she had returned to something resembling normality, going out with him or her friends, returning to work full-time at the leisure centre, he could tell that there was still an absence in her, a hollowing out.

And so he'd decided to propose. Right now, it would cheer her up, give her something to look forward to, focus on. But more than that, he loved her, wanted to spend the rest of his life with her. 'We're barely out of college,' Ronan had said when he told him of his plan. 'What are you, American?' But it felt to Micheál that the time was right.

They were nearing the point where strand met estuary. The walkers had begun to thin out, the team in training would be too far away now to notice a man drop to one knee. He hesitated, feeling again the cool-to-the-touch box in his pocket, the surprisingly sharp edges. He'd taken out a Credit Union loan to cover it. After that initial maternity cover, he'd yet to find a permanent role anywhere, instead subbing or covering in a number of schools throughout the city. With Nadine out of work a lot over the past couple of years, post-surgery, it had been impossible to save. In fact, her parents had often been needed to swoop in and help with the cost of rehab, rent. Still, with her back working full-time now, things were on a more secure footing. And he hoped that, soon, her thoughts would return to physiotherapy, setting up her own clinic. Not that he'd rush her into that.

The remaining walkers ahead of them stopped, doubled back. They were an elderly couple, he saw, as they neared.

Mid-to-late sixties, both speed-walking, arms flailing. The man saluted as they passed. Micheál returned the wave, Nadine too.

'So cute,' she said.

'They are.'

Sand ran into brackish water. Seagulls swooped overhead, lounged in the estuary. Now that the universe had conspired to give him this opportunity – the strand clear for hundreds of metres, the drizzle abated – he felt the familiar spark of anxiety. This was mad. Ronan was right: they were too young. She was going to say no. Of course she was.

Nadine stared across the estuary, at what looked like the ruins of an old castle. He dropped to his knee without her looking, fumbled the box from his pocket.

Opened it.

She was going to say no.

Prepare yourself. Be ready for the pain.

He waited for her to turn, put him out of his misery. Then he realised that she already had turned, was looking down at him, smiling. And her left hand – when had she done that? The glove was gone, skin bared to the elements.

38

He drags the chair out from the kitchen and places it in front of his bedroom window, facing out across the bay. It's one of those unseasonably warm days that feels more like spring than winter. In one hand he has his notebook and blue and red biros; in the other he carries a cup of milky tea, which he places, tilted, on the sill. When he sits, he crosses his legs, rests the notebook on his thigh. Once ready, he flicks the notebook to the next fresh page. With the red biro he writes in the date, time and the information he's already memorised, from the marine website, on the ship in the bay below.

Arklow Rover
Flag: IE
Dest: GB, IPS
13.8/11.9 knots

The creak of the gate alerts him to the visitor. A woman in what looks to be exercise gear is climbing the rise towards the house. Sammy appears from inside and races towards her, tail wagging. Micheál squints. The untethered swing of her arms announces that it is Brenda before she is close enough to tell. Her stride has always had the same wild abandon to it.

'Well, this is a surprise.'

'What? Oh, yeah – a welcome one, I hope.' She laughs. Sammy looks up at both of them, tongue out. 'No, I was just passing and realised that I forgot to mention to you the last day when you were in, like, that I'm having – well, being made have – a little something in The Arms tomorrow night. For my birthday.'

'Twenty-one, I presume?'

'Close, close.' She looks out to the bay – towards the tanker, it seems – then continues: 'Anyway, Mick, I should have said it to you, but d'you know you're more than welcome to come along. Áine will be there, as you probably know –' he did not;

she had said nothing about the party to him when they last spoke – 'and there'll be a few others, and it should be a good night, anyway. You only turn twenty-one once, sure.'

'That's true, alright.' He grins. 'Thanks for the invite, Brenda; I'll definitely try and make it in for it. I mean, I should manage to pop in for one or two, alright, no problem.'

Micheál watches her walk away, Sammy following her as far as the gate. Once she reaches the road, she puts in those white, comma-shaped earphones and gives him a wave. After she's gone from sight, he turns and looks out the bay. The distance between the tanker and Illauntannig appears to have widened since he last looked. It may be a trick of the light or distance or even his failing eyes, but it does seem that the ship is finally picking up speed, forging ahead.

XXXIX

It was Áine who called him. He was in the bathroom at work when he felt the phone vibrate in his pocket. Someone had snuck a furtive drag not too long ago, a smell of smoke holding in the air. Once he saw her name on the screen, though he couldn't explain it, he knew exactly why she was calling.

The postman had found her. She must have known what was happening, as she'd opened the front door before collapsing. He saw her slouched over on the tiles by the kitchen table. An ambulance was called. She was in the Tralee General now, Áine explained, in the ICU. 'You need to get here as fast as you can.'

He left without saying anything to anyone in the staffroom. He thought about ringing Nadine, but held off, as he drove out of the city, thankful for the light mid-morning traffic. She was still on a high from the honeymoon; had even started to talk about physiotherapy again. Their life together finally seemed to be back on track. Maybe the situation wasn't as bad as Áine feared.

A constant, pervasive drumming had filled his ears since the call, and it only stopped after Newcastle West, when Áine rang again and said there was no point rushing.

She was gone.

40

Áine arrives at the house unannounced on the afternoon of Brenda's birthday. She refuses a cup of tea, some Kimberleys, even a seat, as she stands in the kitchen, arms crossed. 'Have you a decision made, Mick?'

'I have,' he says, keeping the table between them.

'And?'

'It's a no, Áine. I'm sorry, but it'd just be dishonest. We'd be like the Lynches when they sold the land to our grandparents. I mean, whoever took it, they'd have no idea what they were really getting.'

Áine sighs. 'Don't be ridiculous, Mick; we're nothing like the Lynches. Look, the time's right. Saoirse and I both want this, you know that. We need it.'

'I know. I'm sorry.'

She leans against the counter by the sink, scratches furiously at her scalp. 'You know, your saying no isn't going to just magically bring an end to this. You get that, right?'

'I do.'

'Mick, I've always thought it was only daughters who turn into their mothers.'

'Ah, come on now.'

A silence falls between them. He had expected Áine to fume, but she instead appears tired. Sammy comes and rests his head on Micheál's feet.

Turning into his mother. What nonsense. Sure, nowadays, he struggles to articulate exactly how he feels about her. To get all the pinballing memories and thoughts and emotions to settle, so he can see how they align. It isn't as clear as it was in his youth – the resentment, or near hatred. Under that: hurt. That she would make him do what she made him do when he was still, really, just a child. But she is his mother. There is love there. And maybe, after his return to the headland, now that he finds himself doing what she did for so long, maybe some respect has come in. Or, if not respect, a sense of solidarity. An understanding of what she went through, doing all this, alone. The compulsion. And why certain sacrifices are necessary.

'You staying down for the party?' he asks.

Áine sighs. 'Yes, Mick, I am.'

'Good, good. She deserves a nice night.'

Áine shakes her head, makes for the still-open front door. Sammy's tail gives a hesitant wag, swishing across the floor. She's at the door before she turns, seems only now to register what he said. 'Are you going to actually come tonight, so?'

'I told her I'd do my best to make it in for one or two if I can.'

'Come, Mick. There'd be no harm in you taking one night off.'

'I know, I know; I'll do my best.'

'I'm sure you will,' she says, closing the door behind her.

XLI

Nadine lost her job first when the recession hit. It was October, ghoulish Halloween decorations already up around the apartment block. Micheál had been teaching full-time in a school in the inner city, and was hoping to be made permanent, but by the following summer they were both out of work. Neither had much chance of finding work elsewhere, not in the current climate. And Nadine's parents could no longer help them with rent or bills. Though he never said anything, it was clear that her father's dealership was struggling. Messages on the envelopes piling up in their apartment from the bank grew bolder, redder, the landlord's voicemails more irate.

It was Nadine's idea, of course. The plan came to her early enough, but he held out, hoping to find another way. What about moving abroad for a year or two? No, she couldn't be that far away from her parents, especially while they were struggling. What about moving in with them for a while? A firm no. She wanted to be close to them, but not too close. Eventually, he had to concede that there were few other options.

He rang Áine, explained the situation. He knew there'd be no real interest in the house and land, not now. Even if there was, they wouldn't get much for it. Certainly not a fair price. It was better to wait until things improved. In the meantime, there was an empty house on hand.

'You can go back if you want, Mick. But you have to tell her.'

'Sure, yeah. I will.'

The relief on Nadine's face was visible when he said they had Áine's blessing to move to the headland. 'It'll give us time to reset and build again,' she said. Things would right themselves in time. Without the pressure of rent and the costs of city living, they should just about get by.

42

Sammy whines as Micheál prepares to leave. 'I won't be long; I'll just stay for one and head away again, okay?' Sammy sniffs at his polished shoes. Micheál gives himself a final once-over in the hallway mirror. The black shirt is the right call. Nadine had always said it was a good colour on him. There was the little nick on his chin from shaving; he must remember to take off the square of toilet paper before he reaches the village.

When he sets off the land is already in darkness, the Paps and wind vanes twirling inland on the Stacks all extinguished. Still, a strong moon is out to guide him, and the calmness of the night means he'll hear cars coming from a long way off, will have plenty of warning.

The land tumbles downwards to sea level as he enters the village. His stomach grumbles again and he hopes it will settle once he is in among them. His pace slows as the pub comes into view. A sprawl of people outside the entrance, smoking and chatting. He recognises most of them, nods as he approaches.

The bar is packed. Micheál feels a tension across his chest, trying to work a route through the crowd. Eyes turn to him, dart away. Someone laughs nearby. On the TV, a white-jerseyed team is playing a red team. He is too far away to tell the score or the name of the teams.

He spots Áine by the bar, shoulders his way towards her. The look of surprise when she sees him appears genuine. It's the way she exaggerates it after a moment, bulging her eyes, bringing her hand to her mouth as if this were a panto, that lets him know she's drunk.

'You actually came.'

'Can I get you anything?'

'Have you changed your mind about the land?'

'Áine, come on. Not here.'

'Then I don't want anything from you, thank you very much.'

She slips off the barstool and meanders her way to the far side of the bar.

The barman is a young lad with hair like a wet mop. The shoulders of his black T-shirt are freckled with dandruff. 'What are you having, sir?' he asks.

'Guinness,' Micheál says.

He flinches as a roar goes up around him, the red team having scored.

Pint in hand, he looks around for Brenda. He spots her cordoned off in a corner booth, surrounded by friends and family and Aengus. She smiles when she sees him, raises her index finger. One minute. He looks around, unsure what to do. He takes a gulp of stout, looks up at the match. He's much closer to the TV now, can see that it's Man United versus Spurs. United are winning 2–1, the first half nearing its end.

'Mick.'

He turns around, towards the call. Sean Scanlon, an old hurling teammate, waves him over. He's standing by the bar in a cluster of lads turned towards the TV. Micheál weaves a way to him, shakes hands, the farmer's hand like sandpaper. There's a lot of grey in his beard. Much like his own now, Micheál supposes, when left to grow.

'Jesus, if it isn't Saint Francis of Assisi himself. How are you keeping, stranger?'

'Grand, yeah. Yourself?'

'Can't complain now.' He taps Micheál's pint glass. 'You'll have another one?'

Micheál looks towards Brenda, still encircled, Aengus's arm draped around her. 'Go on, so.'

He has drained his first pint by the time the second one is handed to him. Sean stands beside him, both of them facing the screen. A Spurs player should equalise, but miskicks and blazes over the crossbar. Sean tilts his head towards Micheál, close enough that he has no need to shout and can't be over-heard. 'Look, I never thanked you, Mick, for that night. I was in a bad way, you know. Thought we were going to lose the farm. I wasn't really thinking.'

The light hadn't gone off that night, Micheál remembers, and Sammy had sensed nothing. It was luck, if anything. A full harvest moon drew his attention out the window in his bedroom, fell like a spotlight on the red Gore-Tex rain jacket Sean had discarded on his way towards the cliffs. When he stepped outside, the moonlight was such that he could easily make out Sean's sitting shape up by the cliff edge. He had no idea how long he'd been there before he noticed.

'No worries, Sean. I'm glad to hear things are better now.'

By the time the second half has started, and he's on his third pint – also bought for him by Sean – he feels the familiar drag start up in him. He looks towards Brenda's table. No sign of her. He glances around the pub, which has emptied out a little. She could be in the toilet. Did she still smoke? She could be outside.

He leaves the pub by the back entrance, which opens on to the laneway that leads from the main street down to the community centre. The place is thick with smokers, more people out here than in the pub now. Brenda is smoking beside the rubbish bins, a few of her old schoolmates with her. Brenda grins when he steps out the door, hugs him, smoke curling up from her fingers.

'You made it.'

'I did promise.'

She steps back, takes a drag from her cigarette. Then she reaches a hand to his chin, plucks away the square of red-dotted toilet paper. Fuck; he'd forgotten all about it. 'That sister of yours has been drinking since she got back from your place, by the way. What's that about?'

'Family stuff, you know.'

'Ye should be on the same side, everything ye've been through.'

'I know.'

She takes another drag, blows smoke out the corner of her mouth. Her friends finish their cigarettes, return inside. He is trying to think of something else to say, to keep her here with him rather than having her return to the party, when Áine appears out the door.

'Ah, Mick, you didn't bring her a present? That's bad form. Not even a token for the woman who's had a crush on you since she was about twelve.'

Brenda reddens. Micheál steps forward. 'Áine, come on now. That's enough of that. You're drunk.'

'I am at that. It's not often I get a night away, after all. From my *family*,' she says, practically spitting the word at him. A finger speared towards Brenda. 'She used to follow you around the house, do you not remember that? And all the time after you left she'd hoover up any news of you. Even the stuff she didn't want to hear. Like Nadine.'

'Enough now, Áine,' Brenda says.

'Anyway, I told her most of everything, Mick. About what you and Mam used to do. The visitors. All those souls you saved. Though the whole fucking headland knows that, even if they like to pretend that they don't. I told her how you left Saoirse and me to it; that you didn't care. Never looked back. Yet still she asked after you. All those years before you came back here. Your grand return. With Nadine.' Her gaze is steady now. Micheál feels his stomach lurch. There is nothing he can do to stop this playing out. 'But that didn't last long, did it? She was gone after a few months. And everyone wondered why. Brenda did, didn't you, Brenda? But the reason for her leaving – that I didn't tell her. God knows why I still showed any kind of loyalty to you. But wouldn't that make a fine present now, Mick? To tell her that.'

'Áine,' Micheál whispers.

His sister turns to Brenda. 'He never told her. All their years together. He even made her move down here and everything, and still he didn't tell her. Didn't warn her. She had to find out for herself, hadn't she, Mick?'

The look on Brenda's face threatens to floor him.

He takes a step back. 'Happy birthday again, Brenda,' he manages to say before turning away from them.

'Mick,' Brenda calls.

'Was it three or four months she was at the time, Mick?' Áine shouts after him.

He turns the corner of the pub. Down on the strand, the tide is almost fully in, nothing but stones visible.

XLIII

It was just easier, at first, not to tell her. He was free from all that stuff, and the last thing he wanted was to dredge it up again. As time passed, it became harder to bring it up; then, in many ways, it seemed best not to tell her at all. He never expected they'd have to spend more than a few hours back on the headland.

As the day of the move approached, he went over the missed opportunities he'd had to tell her. Each of those past moments better options than now. They were too far into their plans to reveal this, too far into their knowing each other for it not to seem like a betrayal. But maybe he was worrying too much anyway. His mother hadn't mentioned the visitors in years. Yes, they tended to avoid the topic, but surely she would have mentioned something, if they were still coming. Áine likewise said nothing. And how long were they going to be there anyway? It was a temporary measure, just until they got back on their feet.

Nadine fell in love with the place as soon as they arrived. 'God, this view.' She picked up some physio work at a clinic in Tralee; Micheál managed to wrangle a few hours subbing in Causeway Comprehensive School. Nadine even started painting classes two evenings a week in Tralee. 'I'm going to do justice to this place,' she declared to him one night as they sat outside the front door, chairs dragged out from the kitchen.

They had been there no more than two months when she told him. 'Terrible timing, I know,' she said, waving the still-wet stick around. A drop of something struck his cheek; he hoped it was just water. His heart was a soaring bird in his chest as he wrapped her up in his arms. 'Jesus,' he said.

Straight away, he declared that she was not allowed do anything. She just had to relax and let him take care of everything. Like after your injury, he almost said. He kept careful track of her doctor appointments, the amount and timing of the supplements she had to take, drove her to her art classes, made sure – after the doctor's recommendation – that she cut down on caffeine. 'I'm doing all the cleaning for the next nine months, too,' he declared. She scoffed. 'What?' he asked. 'Nothing.'

The baby's heartbeat, when he first heard it, reminded him of a washing machine. Or a cartoon train. He still heard the steady, insistent rhythm as he drove Nadine home from the Tralee General, pulled up in front of the closed gate, got out of the car. The sunlight atop the sea gave it a dazzling sheen. He had to squint to take it in. How long had it been now? Nearly four months? And still nothing. Maybe things really had changed. After all, wasn't Ireland a different place now, even in the years since he left? There were more outlets for people who were feeling – well, down. Helplines, support groups, things like that. Without them, wouldn't this be the perfect spot to stay, to make their own, to raise a family?

She'd only been eleven weeks along when it happened. He had a couple of hours in the school that afternoon, so Nadine was by herself when the visitor appeared. By the time Micheál arrived home, he found Nadine sitting among the wildflowers, hysterical. 'I tried to stop him,' she kept saying. 'I kept shouting at him, and I tried to catch up to him.' He brought her inside, put blankets over her and made her drink a double shot of whiskey. The glass trembled in his hand as he brought it to her, knowing now, finally, it would all have to come out.

It was a week later that her calls woke him up from where he was sleeping in Áine's old room. He ran to her, found her hunched over in their bed, her hands to her stomach. 'Something's wrong,' she said. The drive to the hospital in Tralee was achingly long, broken only by her groans and his useless reassurances. After he'd rushed her into the A&E and a porter led her away, he returned to his car, which he'd parked in the ambulance bay, and needed to move. As he went to close the passenger door, he saw the massive stain on the seat, and knew there would be no way it'd ever come off.

Nadine's father appeared in the ward the next day when it was time for her to be discharged. His tone was apologetic, but firm. 'She wants to come home with me, son. You'll need to give her some space, I'm afraid.'

Micheál's hand found the wall, as he looked to steady himself, to quell a sudden sense of spiralling downwards. 'Right, okay.'

44

Micheál hears Sammy barking as he approaches the house. Out of breath, he moves past the house and towards the field. He had practically run all the way from the pub, from Áine's stinging words, from the look on Brenda's face that had struck much deeper. His shins, of all things, ache, and he thinks he has a blister on his heel. He surveys the field. The long grass stands tall, untrammelled. In the darkness, all colour has drained from the field. Out to sea, a ship flares near the horizon, on the verge of falling out of sight.

PART THREE

45

Through binoculars Micheál watches a huddled jury of barnacle geese congregate near the cliffs, honking, eating grass, weeds, wildflowers like the common dog violet, which has flowered a month earlier than usual. Perhaps it signalled an early spring. Not that there'd been much of a winter, Micheál thinks, lying on the Garfield mattress. Storms, yes, but little real cold. He'd only been forced to put the fire on a handful of times, the sack of coal he'd ordered last September still near full. He stifles a yawn. If he'd managed an hour's sleep last night it didn't feel like it.

The geese take flight as one and a moment later Micheál hears a van's high-pitched struggle with the incline to the house. He checks his phone: 10.15 a.m. He'd booked the 11–1 slot, had hoped to have at least another hour watching the birds. Before descending the Stira, he guides the thin hands of the porcelain-dish clock until they match the time in his own grip.

Downstairs, with Sammy beside him, tail sweeping the air, he opens the front door. The delivery van is parked directly outside, its side door slid wide. The delivery man stands at the open space, curly black hair tousled by the sea breeze;

with difficulty, he lifts two cardboard boxes of food and turns towards the house.

'Morning,' he says. 'Mr Burns, is it?'

Micheál nods.

'Where'll I put them?'

'You can just throw them up on the table inside,' he says, making way for him. Sammy sniffs at the man's trouser leg as he passes.

'You made good time, anyway.'

'Yeah, there was a last-minute cancellation, so you got bumped up the order. Hope that's okay?'

'Oh, yeah, no problem,' he says, the earlier frustration now gone. In its place was a different feeling, one that surprised him: a longing for company. He hadn't spoken to a soul since he'd called into the post office in Ballyheigue last week to collect his dole.

The delivery man carries in the final box, dog food at the top. Though he can't see it from where he stands, Sammy must sense it, as he eyes the box with an intense, almost fierce longing.

'That's it,' the man announces.

'Great stuff. Here, do you fancy a cup of tea before you take off? A scone or something?'

The delivery man frowns by the door. 'Ah, no, I better keep going. I've another couple of deliveries to make before lunch.' His light-natured tone fails to hide a deeper awkwardness. Behind him, Micheál can see into the van, its bareness exposed.

After the van drives away, he begins to unpack the boxes. He'd gotten more food than the previous order, and that had done him for three weeks. This should get him through a whole month. Looking back, using Brenda's shop two-to-three times a week had made no sense. It cost him more money and meant he spent extra time away from the cliffs. And it's not like Brenda's shop was struggling; she had a legion of loyal customers. Things were easier this way. The only person who would give out to him about this was Áine, but they hadn't spoken since the party either. She didn't even call on his birthday last week. Forty-two. Same age as his father when his thick-valved heart took him from them. The only communication from her, which had been sent indirectly, was the letter sitting open on the counter by the sink.

The leadenness that held him after Nadine, he can feel it on the edges of himself now, like a sheet waiting to settle to his form. If it settles, he knows, it'll turn to granite, encase him. But he does not know how to shift it.

Maybe resolving things with Áine would help, but she refused to understand his reasons for not wanting to sell. The obligation he has.

Sammy's gaze hasn't left the box that contains the dog food. Micheál sighs. 'Alright, I'll give you half now, but you're not getting the other half till lunch.' Sammy lets out a little yelp, which he takes as agreement.

After feeding Sammy and putting away the rest of the delivery, he checks the time: 11.04. He could return to the attic and get another couple of hours of birdwatching in before lunch. As he makes for the hallway, and the Stira, he glances out the road-facing window. The gate is open. The delivery man mustn't have bothered to shut it. He weighs up whether to close the gate now or wait till lunch. He sighs. He might as well get it over with.

Outside, the wind swirls in a way that it often does here, as if unable to choose a direction in which to go. It can sometimes feel like you're being buffeted from all sides. Habit more than anything makes Micheál look in the direction of the cliffs. The figure stands out, not against long grass or the hard rock near the cliffs, but against the cold steel of sky. They have no more land on which to climb.

XLVI

He never called Nadine after she left. Neither did he travel to her parents' house, where she stayed those first weeks and months. What was the point, after what had happened? Even if he did somehow convince her to return, the trust was gone. Too much was gone.

Everything fell apart in the aftermath. He stopped leaving the house except when absolutely necessary. The weight of losing her made every action an effort. Time turned hazy, every day passing in a fog of lying on the couch, watching *The Big Bang Theory, Two and a Half Men, King of Queens* – half-hour sitcoms on loops, allowing him to shut off his mind to everything but the laugh track. Nights stretched and blurred, staring at the ceiling until he eventually gave up and returned to the couch, channel-surfing for anything that would tune out his thoughts.

Áine visited a lot during this time. Their relationship had

softened somewhat since he helped with her loan application, but maybe this was him being cynical. Meeting her for lunch in the village was one of the few times he forced himself to leave the house. She never berated him for what he'd done, or not done; instead, she filled him in on her own life, which was coming together as quickly as his had disintegrated – her new job at the tax office in Cork city, her engagement to Brian. She asked how he was doing: was he exercising? Was he eating well? How was he feeling? One weekend, she appeared with an open cardboard box in her back seat. A surprise, she said. He heard the sound of the tiny tail slapping cardboard as she opened the car door.

'I figured you could use a bit of company out there,' she said.

Micheál put his hand near the pup's face, allowed him to take in his scent.

'Thanks, Áine. He's a beaut.'

'It's no trouble, Mick. No trouble at all.'

Sammy's presence shook him somewhat from his torpor, forcing him out of the house for walks, introducing a pattern to the day. But the thing that brought him back to himself was Tadhg Kennedy. He doesn't remember the names of all the visitors – some never even give one – but he remembers his. Tadhg was the first visitor he had to deal with after Nadine's departure. His first visitor since he'd left the headland over a decade earlier.

It was magic hour when he passed by the window; Micheál only spotted him as he was at the counter by the sink, reaching into the press for Sammy's dog food. He had no idea where the flashlight could be found, forgot to grab a fleece or coat as he ran after him. He remembers a seagull mewing overhead as he ran through the wildflowers, its lonesome shriek.

A tall, rangy man, balding, with a raised cyst on the exposed part of his head, he looked in his mid-to-late forties. He gave off an air of general weariness, sitting at the cliff edge, his legs already dangling. He had walked all the way from Tralee, he revealed once he started talking, an hour after Micheál positioned himself near him, a few metres from the edge. He had lost his job, was in crippling debt. He had yet to reveal to his wife the full extent of their trouble. It had gotten to the point where he made sure to rise before her in the mornings, to scoop up the post as soon as it was stuffed through the post box. He hid the bills in his home office, in a binder marked 'Tax Files 2004'. Tadhg rubbed at his eyes, pulled a handful of grass from the earth. One quick shuffle and he'd be gone, Micheál thought, and checked again that he was still close enough to snatch at him should he look to fall. 'The thing is, I get so angry at her when she asks about this stuff, when she offers to help. All I can do is shout at her and say it's fine, it's all fine. How shite is that of me?'

After Tadhg's wife, Barbara, had collected him, Micheál sat by the kitchen table, waiting for his mind to catch up with what he'd just experienced. Stained sheets of newspaper decorated the floor where Sammy had pissed. During the visit, he'd felt alert, focused, so unlike how he'd been feeling the past few months, even if things had improved somewhat with Sammy's arrival. Though he refused to name it even to himself, he knew what was coursing through him.

He remembered a game for Ballyheigue Under-12s against Lixnaw, undoubtedly his best game for the club before he was forced to quit. He'd played centre forward that day, a gale coming in off the bay. He'd already scored 1–4 from play as the game entered the final few minutes. Lixnaw – the previous year's county champions – were ahead by two points. It was Tuan who pucked the sliotar out from the full-back line. Micheál sensed that it would hang in the air that bit longer, caught by the wind, so he slipped behind his marker. The sliotar landed ahead of him, leaving him one-on-one with the goalie. He has relived this moment countless times in the years since: the effortless flick of the sliotar up into the air with his hurley, landing on its face; the slap of his marker's hurley against his arm, trying to put him off, the goalie closing the distance between them; how Micheál pivoted left, struck the sliotar past the goalie and into the net. The winning score. Afterwards, teammates swamped him. Ger O'Mahony, the bainisteoir, gave him a bear hug.

Though he knows that everyone there that day has likely forgotten that moment, he still remembers the feeling afterwards, and it is how he felt after stopping Tadhg Kennedy from jumping off the cliffs. It was the first time he'd saved someone alone, the first time it hadn't all been jumbled with resentments, fears, thoughts of escape. After all, what had he to escape to now? He had failed spectacularly at life. Here, at least, was purpose.

47

This time he has yet to find the hook. He's unsure how much time has passed since he came up here, though it must be a couple of hours as the sun has moved from high inland to skirt the summit of Caherconree across the bay. At this time of year the sun always uses the peninsula opposite as a landing strip, coming to rest behind Mount Brandon further west, setting the mountains ablaze on a clear evening.

The woman, in her early-to-mid sixties, he guesses, sits at the cliff edge, the cries and challenges of gannets nesting in the crevices of the cliff carrying up to them. She is a short, slim figure with a face of sharp angles, a chasm of a wrinkle between the brows suggesting a lifetime of furrowed thought. She is wearing black chino trousers and loafers, stylish glasses with red-flecked rims that match her double-breasted mac. She looks like she has just stepped out of an office – he wants to say an architectural firm, or maybe a solicitors' – for a long lunch.

Micheál sits about ten feet away from her, further along the cliff, and a little in from the edge. As usual, Sammy has done a much better job of forming a connection, lying beside her, the woman's hand absently running through his fur. Helena. He'd gotten that much out of her when he first approached, careful to keep his distance, his body language open, placating. 'Is it alright if I can come closer so we can talk?' he'd asked. It was important that it be their decision. After she nodded, he'd moved closer, sat on a patch of sea thrift. 'I'm here for you,' he added. 'I'm here to listen.' He used to say 'to help' when he first started, but his mother told him to never use that word with a visitor. When someone had already made it to the cliff edge, they felt beyond help, she explained. All you could be was a good listener, a kind ear. If you got them talking, sooner or later their problems would spill out – so it was about getting to that moment of connection.

But the woman wasn't talking. He has allowed the silence to sit for long stretches. He has tried hooking her with different subjects – how stressful work can be nowadays, how difficult it can be to be alone, how loss can seem crushing in the short-term – but none of them has worked. And since he first rushed up here she has been calm, almost serene. He knows this to be a bad sign. There is nothing impulsive about her being here; she has come to a decision and made peace with it. These are often the hardest visitors to turn around.

'My sisters hate me,' he finds himself saying. And it all comes out of him then: how they want to sell the land but he has refused; the fight in the pub on Brenda's birthday; the letter that arrived a couple of weeks later, a solicitor's letter, not sent by Áine but at her direction. They are aiming to push ahead the sale with or without his agreement. 'They want to be rid of it,' he says. He still feels congested, and Helena has yet to acknowledge his words, so he keeps talking: about growing up here, the visitors, about coming back to this place with Nadine, what he failed to tell her, how she left. The only thing he withholds is the baby.

The horizon is a blurred blotch of red and blue by the time he's finished. Her expression when he wipes his eyes and looks at her makes him momentarily want to jump off the cliff, just to be away from the pity of it. But at least she is looking at him.

'I'd like to go down now,' she says.

Micheál hesitates, unsure what she means by 'down', but when she swivels her legs back in from the edge, stands and begins walking downhill, he rises, relieved. He catches up with her, sees that her expression remains hard to read. At least she is away from the cliff edge, he thinks, as Sammy lopes ahead, startling a bird – a thrush, or maybe a redwing – from the undergrowth.

XLVIII

Micheál remembers a conversation with his mother, after a visit. The two of them stood by the kitchen table, soaked and freezing, the kettle a rising grumble behind them.

'Change out of your clothes, then come back down and I'll have a cup of tea ready for you,' she said.

Micheál retreated down the hallway. His hands refused to stop shaking; he couldn't even grasp the zip on his jacket, his fingers were so numb. Áine's bedroom door opened as he passed; a shadow peeked out.

'Go back to bed,' he said. Then he stopped and turned to her. 'Can you unzip this, please?'

Áine stepped out into the hallway, nightshirt down past her knees. Her lips pursed as she unzipped his mac.

'Thanks,' he said, hurrying towards his room.

Once back in the kitchen, in dry clothes, a quilt wrapped

shawl-like around him, he sat opposite his mother. She still wore her outdoor gear, her fringe matted to her forehead. She seemed not to notice, or was simply beyond caring. Her cup of tea – black, no sugar – remained untouched on the table, whereas Micheál cradled his in both hands, even though it felt near-scalding.

'Do you want to stop helping me, Micheál?'

'Sorry?'

'I can see that your heart's not in it anymore, love; and, to be fair, it is asking an awful lot of you, I know that.'

Micheál felt a slight pulse of hope. 'But would you not mind?'

She smiled. 'No, love, of course not.'

'But you always said there needed to be two.'

'I did, I did.' She reached for her cup, finally, took a sip. 'And there would still need to be two, of course.'

'What do you mean?'

'Well, your sister has asked a number of times if she can help.'

'Áine?'

'Yes, of course. Saoirse is far too young. And Áine's older now than you were when you started helping me. She'll be more than able, I'm sure, if you want to step aside.'

He frowned, placed the cup on the table. 'No, no, it's okay; I can keep going.'

'You're sure?'

'Yeah.'

He told himself at the time that he continued to help his mother so as to save his sister from the experience. But deep down he knows that, at least in part, it was due to a petty, rivalrous instinct not to let Áine win.

'Good, love. You're a good boy; I'm so proud of you.'

With that, she rose, poured her near-full cup of tea into the sink and went to change out of her wet clothes.

49

Inside, Micheál leads her to the couch. She looks tired, a touch grey, as if she has only now realised what the last few hours involved. Sammy hops on to the couch, curls up beside her, and Micheál has never been so proud of that beautiful beast.

As he flicks the kettle to boil, he feels an unsettling churn of vulnerability in his chest. Normally, he is the one who has listened to their story, tried to understand it and, if possible, defuse it of some of its power. Yet he still hardly knows anything about this woman, with whom he has shared his own story. It has him off balance.

The kettle rising to a whine, he moves along the sideboard and takes the bottle of Jameson out from the cupboard over the toaster. He rinses two glasses that had been sitting among stained bowls and plates in the sink, fills one with a shot of the whiskey, and downs it. The burn is welcome.

Kettle boiled, he brings Helena a cup of tea and half-measure of whiskey. A second round trip is needed to carry a jug of milk and a chipped bowl of sugar. 'Fire away with that there. Whatever you fancy.'

'Oh, thank you,' she says, though she reaches for neither drink, instead continuing to rub Sammy.

Now that the tension of the afternoon has passed, his stomach gives a sudden reminder that he has skipped lunch.

'Would you like some food, maybe?'

'Food?' she parrots, as if she's never heard of such a thing.

'Yeah, just a bite to eat. It might bring you back to yourself a little.'

She laughs, seeming to find the idea funny. 'Food sounds good,' she says.

The delivery had certainly come at the right time, Micheál thinks, as he returns to the kitchen. There had been little food left in the house, except for turned milk, a couple of potatoes that had sprouted, some frozen peas and a knob of Kerrygold. Any red or tough meat is out for the meal as they'd require her to use a sharp knife. There are salmon darnes in the fridge – them and some mash and frozen peas would do the job, he reckons. He lays the salmon out under the grill, skins the spuds, chops them and drops them into a pot of boiling water. The peas can wait; they'll only need a few minutes to cook.

Helena appears beside him. He starts.

'Oh, sorry,' she says, noticing his shock.

'No, no, you're fine. I was in a world of my own.'

'The bathroom?' she enquires.

Micheál performs a quick mental sweep of the bathroom. The window is locked; his shaver is in his bedroom. There is the mirror, of course, but he would hear that smash, would be able to break down the door before she managed to use it.

'Second door on the right.'

Sammy follows her as far as the bathroom door, then sits outside, as if standing guard. 'You've made a new friend, have you?' Sammy ignores the question, eyes remaining on the bathroom door. 'I'm not jealous,' he whispers. After a quick stir of the potatoes, he glances towards the coffee table, sees that the whiskey has been drunk. He tops it up for her return.

The darnes are a little overcooked and a touch dry, but other than that the meal turns out well. Helena sits opposite him, spreading some butter on to the mash. He had thought he heard her crying at one point in the bathroom, but since re-emerging she has seemed more settled.

He decides to chance a question.

'Is there anyone I can call, Helena? Anyone who might be worrying where you are? Or anyone who can help you get home?'

'No, not anymore, I'm afraid.'

'I'm sorry,' he says.

'You've nothing to be sorry for, Micheál.'

He wonders when he last heard someone say his own name to him. Not since the party, he supposes.

After dinner, little of which is eaten, she asks if there is somewhere she can rest awhile. 'I've had a long day,' she says, allowing herself a half smile.

'Of course,' Micheál says, leading her to the visitors' room. He made sure to wash the sheets after Luke McCarthy, even though it had been a brief stay. She sits on the side of the bed and sighs, looking twenty years older than she'd done minutes earlier. 'I just need a good night's sleep,' she says. 'Like yourself, I think.'

He feels himself blush.

In the kitchen, Micheál turns the armchair around so it's facing the hallway. In some cases, when he's sure the threat from the cliffs has passed, he would spend the night in his own bed, confident that all will be well in the morning. In this case, though, he remains unsure. Her change of mind had been so sudden, so complete; visits usually tended to turn in slower, more meandering ways. It's possible that she simply couldn't jump with him there, disliked the idea of a witness, and so would try to return during the night. Micheál picks up a book from the coffee table, his latest mobile-library read: *History of a Kingdom: Kerry 1699–1999*. He is unlikely to sleep tonight, anyway.

L

A couple of years after Micheál's return, Uncle Dinny took to visiting the headland. In Micheál's youth, Dinny was very much 'the cool uncle', with his long hair, sideburns, denim jacket and motorbike. Micheál remembers it as a sharp red, being lifted atop it at a young age. He had once overheard his mother say Dinny was 'off the rails', that he needed 'to slow down', and even then Micheál sensed that it had nothing to do with how he rode his motorbike. That Dinny seemed gone when he visited Micheál now, along with the denim and hair. He'd replaced the motorbike with a dark-green, second-hand Fiat Punto. After struggling to hold down a job through most of his life, he'd spent the last number of years working as a groundskeeper at Micheál's old school, The Green.

Micheál had seen little of him, really, throughout his childhood, and was unsure why he'd taken to visiting now, but he was grateful for the company, the distraction. And

Dinny liked to talk of the family's past, which interested Micheál, as he knew so little about it: 'You never met our father, your grandfather, of course, but he was a distant man in most ways. Not a disciplinarian, mind – he left the wooden spooning and all that stuff to our mother – but, I suppose, there was always a remove with him. Maybe it was his job, you could tell that many around town steered clear of him when given the opportunity. It was more a coldness than an anger or dislike or anything like that; like he didn't much care either way what you did, so long as you didn't bring the family into disrepute. The only time you'd see him animated, really, was at a Stacks or Kerry game. I often think I got into the football only to see that side of him, d'you know? To bring it out of him.'

After a few visits, Micheál found himself directing Dinny's reminiscences towards his mother. What was she like growing up? 'She was quiet, but there was a steeliness to her, and a bit of mischief too at times. I remember the Sullivans – they would have been next door to us, growing up – built a snowman one winter in their back garden, but one afternoon while they were out, Aileen snuck in and pulverised the poor thing. There was nothing left of it by the time the Sullivans got back, catching her at the end of the act. I never really understood why she did that. But, then, she always liked helping people too, your mother. I remember her thinking about getting into nursing before going the teacher route. And we had this neighbour, Mr Shaw, who had a problem with his leg – I forget what it was – but he had a cane, and he used to snail about everywhere. Every Sunday, Aileen would walk with him to Mass, and back again afterwards. It wasn't on anyone's prompting either; she just saw him struggling and decided to do it. She'd do some errands for him too, now and again.'

After Dinny left that day, it wasn't the image of his mother helping Mr Shaw that stayed with Micheál, that he returned to time and time again, but that of her in the Sullivans' back yard, battering and stamping a snowman out of existence. He imagined her, brazen-faced, staring down the Sullivans upon their return. An absence of regret, contrition.

On another visit, he asked Dinny how she met his father. 'She went all the way to Limerick to meet a Tralee lad; funny that. Interesting that you ended up going the same route, isn't it, lad? The teaching. I knew him from the club, your dad. He was four years older than me, of course, like your mam, but I would have watched him play before he left for the teaching college – he was Minor level, maybe on the Under-21s. A tough footballer, your dad; built like a bull – like yourself, I see – and had a deceptive step of speed on him.

'She was besotted, your mother; that I remember. She brought him home at one point; they must have been seeing each other a year or so, and so he was wheeled in to the family – or at least myself, Sheila, and the parents; Mikey had already moved to London – for inspection. To make it official, I suppose. We received him in the kitchen – this was the old house in St John's Park in town now, remember – which was cramped, with this circular wooden table plonked atop sticky lino. My mother, bless her, had the good plates out, cutlery too. And with all of us crowded in there, it felt more like a cell or, d'you know, one of those interrogation rooms you'd see in the cop shows on TV. And maybe that's how the da wanted it, being in his element, d'you know, because as soon as he was seated he started bombarding your poor father with questions. Shane, he looked exhausted by the end of it. Only then did my mother start offering out the tea, bit of grub. Though, even then, the da, before the pot made it to Shane, he asked him, "Would you like a bottle of stout instead? I've a couple left from Christmas." But Shane shook his head, said the tea would do him. And this seemed to satisfy the da, like Shane had passed one final test, and he turned to my mother, and said, "Give the man his tea; can't you see that he's parched?"'

Once, Micheál broached the subject of the visitors with Dinny. 'Your mother told me about it first, told me what Mam had told her shortly after they moved out here. I think they hoped it was just a once off, but when the second one jumped, there could be no doubting it, that the place just had that mark on it. Certain places just have certain moods to them, d'you know – I mean, there's a reason why they call them black spots, don't they? And this was one of those, no doubt about it.' He looked away from Micheál. 'As you well know by now, of course.'

Did either of Micheál's parents explain why they decided to move out to the headland? 'No, never gave a reason; though I never asked. Just thought that was Aileen, being the dutiful one. We didn't really talk about the visitors then; it was left under the floorboards, d'you know? But she obviously knew what she was letting herself in for. But she went, anyway. I don't know, maybe she went because of them too. Even then she likely thought she was doing good, doing God's work. Funny how good Christian work, even when there is legitimate good done, often has a kick to it, d'you know?

'And then, before I knew it, a few years had passed and your dad died, and I did try to be there for your mother, I did try – and I was there a bit, if you remember; I did come out the odd bit, as I knew she was struggling – but I also know that I wasn't there near enough. Not at the time, and not after. And I'm sorry for that, lad; I know I failed you and the girls, and Aileen, for that. Hell, I knew it at the time. And the knowing but not accepting led me down darker roads.

'Honestly, it wasn't till I crashed the bike one day, driving back drunk from Ballybunion, that I started to get my act together, scared off the drink – some bit, anyway – got the job in The Green. Not that it was all straightforward. It was about a year later that I gave the drink up altogether. I don't know, it was like a tap slowly turning off. People who say these things hit you in a moment and you're suddenly another way, I don't know if I believe that; but it was a turning point, the crash – just a gentle curve rather than a sharp bend, if you get me. Anyway, your mother and I hadn't seen each other in a while by that point; her because she refused to leave the headland; me because I felt shitty for not being there for her enough after your father passed. Of course, continuing to stay away wasn't the way to make that right – only made it worse – but it had gotten to the point where I felt unable to face her, or you and your sisters. But I was still on that gentle curve, mostly through it, and so I decided I had to face her. So I drove out, still on the motorcycle, which I'd had repaired. I hadn't quite been able to get rid of it yet, though the thought had repeatedly arisen – as I said, I was still on that curve, not fully through it yet.

'You and your sisters were gone by then, off to your separate corners of the globe, not that I can blame ye. So of course she was on her own when I got there. Jesus, she looked old; I mean, I haven't aged well, for obvious reasons, but neither had she, though I suppose that's for very obvious reasons too. She answered the door with almost a wary look on her; I'd say not many came to the door, and the visitors would hardly knock on their way past. I didn't expect the hug, to be honest, but she gave it, as well as a tired sort of smile. "It's good to see you, Din." I remember struggling to really meet her eyes, I felt so bad, d'you know. Think I mumbled out a "Sorry it's been so long" or something like that, but she just talked over me, said, "Come in, come in." The place was spotless, I remember that. She did a much better job of keeping the place in good nick, no offence, lad – not that I can throw stones, of course. She took to calling me "Binny" for a time after seeing the state of my bedsit.

'It's strange, sitting opposite someone you know so well but haven't seen in a long spell. You know exactly who they were, but are less certain as to who they are, if you get me. It was like that with Aileen. The Aileen I knew was still there, of course, but over that, almost like padding or something, was this new flinty layer, a hardness – that's not exactly the right word – maybe a purposefulness? Is that even a word? It was like she was on a mission or something, is what I'm trying to say. She had this air of being switched on, though under that I could tell that the battery was almost run out. Running on fumes, as they say.

'I visited regularly after that, maybe once a fortnight. I knew she'd no one else, really, bar the visitors, though Áine did come as far as Ballyheigue maybe once a month. And you showed your face once in a blue moon, at least for a while. Don't get me wrong, I understand why ye kept your distance; though she never said it outright, I guessed what she'd done, dragging ye into it. Once, after a few visits, she asked me if I'd want to stay with her for a bit, take one of the spare rooms. "You can come and go as you please," she said. She was lonely, I think, and would have liked the company, but she did also mention about "helping around the place" a bit, if I did stay. And, look, I had to be straight with her, said if I stayed out here, with what happens, I'd be back on the drink within a fortnight. I just couldn't do it; I knew I wasn't able. And she accepted that. I think she always felt that it was too much of a weight by itself, a burden; she needed help carrying the load. Not that that excuses what she did, dragging ye into it so young; I'm not saying that at all. Just that maybe it explains it a little. Though maybe it doesn't either. Our conversations tended to steer clear of these things. She talked about your father a lot; it was obvious, even then, that she still missed him.'

After a few more visits, maybe Micheál grew a little too insistent or pestering in his questions, wanting too much detail, seemingly insignificant things. What music did she listen to growing up? He remembered The Monkees, because she loved their TV show, when she was young – or maybe that was Sheila. And might she have had a thing for Queen too? Micheál nodded. There was a *Best Of* album that she liked to play as she cleaned. He has a clear shot of a memory of her singing 'Bohemian Rhapsody' at the sink, and his looking up at her, laughing at her attempts with the different voices. What was her favourite colour? 'Blue, I think. Yeah, because bluebells were her favourite flowers. And oh yeah, Joni Mitchell – she was mad for her, at one point, just before she went off to Limerick. Playing *Blue* on repeat on the vinyl player in the sitting room.'

He could sense Dinny's growing unease with these questions: the sheer amount of them, the probing follow-ups, the intensity with which Micheál listened. His uncle tried to steer them away from talk of family history, his sister, instead talking about how he felt Kerry would do in this year's All-Ireland, whether Dublin could be stopped and if Éamonn Fitzmaurice was the right man for the job at all. And what was the story with Man United? They'd been a basket case since Fergie left. Each time, Micheál looked to wrestle the conversation back to his mother.

In the end, Dinny stopped coming. Micheál later heard from Áine that he stayed away as he felt that his visits were doing Micheál more bad than good. 'Just seemed to be stirring up stuff that is better off staying still,' he said.

51

Micheál wakes to the sound of nearby crashing. On instinct, he rises from the armchair, braces himself – whether to dive for cover or tackle, in the moment he cannot say. Helena is kneeling under the sink, the press open, frying pan and a pot sprawled on the floor. 'I was going to make you some breakfast,' she says, picking up the frying pan. Arranged on the sideboard is a packet of eggs, rashers, Denny's sausages. 'I thought I'd get more of a start on it before waking you.'

Micheál places a hand back on the chair, steadies himself, a bout of dizziness gripping him after he stood up so fast. 'You're fine. I'm not much of a deep sleeper, these days,' he says. Sammy is already awake, he notices, sitting close to Helena, gaze fixed on the sausages. 'You're feeling well?' he asks.

'I am, much better,' she says, offering a sheepish smile.

Micheál excuses himself and walks down the hallway to the bathroom. He takes a piss, the colour of the stream a coppery amber, reminding him once again that he needs to drink more water. Nadine had plagued him about hydration. He is surprised he'd nodded off; he'd stayed up until the early hours, reading. The last time he remembers checking the clock was a little after four. He'd left the TV alone, in case it woke Helena. At the bathroom sink, he makes a cup of his hands, fills them with water, and buries his face in them.

It is a strange sight to see someone cooking in this kitchen. She seems absorbed in the task, so he leaves her to it and goes about setting the table for the meal, the smell of which has begun to fill the room. Seeming to realise this, Helena reaches over to the window, turns the handle, pushes it open. Her attention is drawn to the radio on the sill.

'Do you mind?'

'Not at all.'

'I've always liked listening to the radio while cooking.'

The radio is switched to RTÉ Radio 1 and as the morning headlines are relayed Micheál wonders how she must feel, listening to news of a day she did not expect to see.

He is unsure if it's the way she cooked the food, or if it's just because he didn't cook it himself, but the breakfast is delicious.

'Glad to hear it,' she smiles as he mumbles his thanks through the last bit of sausage. Sammy, sprawled beside her chair, chews a piece of rasher. She has tried to be furtive, but he's noticed her give most of her portion to the dog.

'We used to holiday here every summer when I was a child,' she says, eyes cast over his shoulder – at the bay out the window, he presumes, the mountains beyond. 'My parents owned a holiday home just outside the village on the headland road. My sister, Cathy, and I used to count down the days every year till it was time to come here. It's so many years ago now. I know memory plays tricks, but, looking back, it feels like we spent every day on the strand, or gallivanting through the dunes. We used to go down to the Black Rock, I remember. It seemed to take an eternity to walk there. We'd catch the little fish in the rock pools, stranded there when the tide retreated. We used to put them in jars, bring them back to live with us in the holiday home.'

'That sounds lovely,' Micheál says. It is the most she has spoken since arriving, and he is now sure that her accent is the soft, reserved variety usually found in south Dublin, though it's not so much an accent of geography as of class. It reminds him, a little, of his mother's phone voice.

'It was. A lifetime ago now, of course.'

'Doesn't make it any less real.'

'No, I suppose not.'

Amid the lull, the weather report comes on the radio. The forecaster warns of another impending storm – this one named Jerome – due in the following morning. Red alert for all counties, the report warns. It is already reaching record wind speeds for a storm this far north in the Atlantic.

'They'll run out of alphabet soon, with all these storms,' he says.

'It seems to be the norm now, alright.'

A sudden thought brings Micheál to his feet. Candles. He'd run out of candles during the last storm and had meant to order more in that delivery. He stalks to the press by the fridge where he keeps things like spare batteries, a lighter, spare biros, measuring tape. After rifling through it, he lets out a low curse. He'd forgotten them. If the storm was as bad as the report suggested, he was sure to need them.

Helena gives him a quizzical look when he turns around.

'Out of candles,' he explains.

Micheál considers cycling into the village to get the candles. He could always go to Costcutter or Centra. Brenda would be unlikely to see him cycle past. But something about shopping at one of her rivals sits awkwardly with him; he can't do it to her. The online orders were different, as they were coming all the way from Tralee. It'd be much worse to shop elsewhere in the village. But then he stops himself: he can't leave Helena alone here anyway.

As if he has been thinking aloud, Helena makes a sudden offer: 'I could go into the village for you, if you'd like? I can get you those candles?' When he hesitates, she adds, 'It'll do me good, I think; help clear my head.'

He imagines her turning left down on the road, jumping by the fort. He sees her walking along the strand in Ballyheigue, making it as far as the Black Rock and wading out into the sea. But she has seemed much clearer this morning, a spark in her that had been absent the day before. And it is always like this, anyway, when there is no one to take a visitor away – this frayed moment of leave-taking. Though, in this case, she has promised to return.

'I have a bike around the side of the house,' he says.

'Perfect.' Helena smiles.

LII

One visitor, when Micheál was fourteen or fifteen, arrived during a storm. Sometimes the rise of the cliff can protect the house from the worst of the conditions, but that night the wind was coming across the bay, buffeting the front of the house.

His mother, on lookout, spotted the visitor staggering towards the cliffs, a raincoat on him, though the hood bobbed uselessly behind him. She had Micheál put on extra layers and wet gear before heading out, but it made little difference, given the force of the deluge and the amount of time spent outside.

The next day his mother let him stay home from school. He slept beyond lunch, then woke shivering. His mother's hand was an ice pack on his forehead, simultaneously unpleasant and welcome. 'Bit of a temperature, alright,' she assessed.

Within a day, it had spread to his throat and chest. He would fall asleep, only for an insistent wheeze, catching in his chest, to wake him and force him on to his side, where he'd lean out of the bed, cough and spit phlegm into a saucepan placed on the floor by his mother. The content grew greener by the day.

The GP made a house call. Bronchitis. A week off school, minimum. He'd have felt elated if he had any energy.

His mother decided to take the week off work. 'Just until you're over the worst of it,' she said. She checked on him often, hand to forehead, asked if he needed anything. She brought him tea, honey, dried toast when he felt up to it – though the toast hurt his throat. She took the saucepan out whenever she left the room, would always bring it back, washed clean. Sometimes, she brought a chair in from the kitchen and sat with him, a book in hand. He resented this intrusion at first, but after a while grew to like it. Her closeness, her watching out for him.

Despite her attention and care, Micheál knew that she did not stay at home during this period solely for him. It was for them, too. And not even them, necessarily, but the chance of them, the faint possibility that someone might show up in daylight. He saw it in the way she sat at an angle to his bed, so she could get a better view out his window; the way she would often leave his room and do her usual checks – look down towards the road from the kitchen, the stepping outside the front door to take a look up into the field and towards the cliff. Sometimes she would even check around the back of the house, in case someone was hiding there, waiting for her to return inside before bolting up through the field.

But at least after her checks she would return to his bedside, cool his forehead with her palm, reassure him with a 'Not as bad as yesterday,' or a 'You're getting there,' and take her seat beside him again. 'Sleep, my Superman. Sleep.' And so he did.

53

Helena cycles out of sight under a sky so vibrant it seems native to a different land. The pinks and reds are sharp enough that he knows others would give them different names – words like 'fuchsia' and 'scarlet'– to do them justice. Still, for all its beauty, he understands that the sky is a harbinger.

Micheál turns from the window, eager to keep hands and mind busy. He clears the table, wipes it with a damp cloth, collecting the crumbs and other food bits in his palm when he slides them off the table. Sammy waits nearby, ready to inspect anything that makes it to the floor. Micheál had offered Sammy's companionship on Helena's cycle into the village. 'He likes the exercise,' he said.

'No, there's no need for that,' she said, already on the bike, the hill down to the gate before them. 'I won't be long.'

Kettle boiled, he pours it into the sink, already filled with ware from this morning, but also the past week. He scrubs at caked-on dirt, some of it stubbornly refusing to wash away. 'She'll be fine. She'll be back before we know it,' he says. He looks around for Sammy to provide affirmation, but the dog is under the kitchen table, sniffing for scraps.

It should take her about half an hour to cycle to the village. He had told her to go to Brenda's shop and wonders now what might happen when she arrives. Might Brenda try and draw

Helena into a conversation, ask what she is doing, where she is staying? Might she recognise the bike propped outside the shop window? Or might Helena recognise her as the woman from his cliff-top confession. He can't remember if he said her name, told her that she ran the shop in the village. 'He saved me; he can't be a bad person,' he imagines her saying to Brenda. His cheeks flush with shame at the thought, the idea, that maybe, on some level, this is why he allowed her to get the candles.

Ware washed, he looks around the kitchen. Maybe he should clean up before Helena returns; it seems likely now that she might stay here a few days, maybe longer. He unearths supplies from beneath the sink, starts in first on the sideboard, scrubbing with the same ferocity that he'd shown earlier to the ware. At one point, he has to stop, another bout of dizziness coming over him. He must be putting too much of himself into the effort.

After he finishes brushing the floor, he looks up at the clock and realises how much time has passed. Outside, the earlier signal fire of a sky has returned to its normal, muted grey. The wind is building.

She should be back by now. Certainly if she were to cycle straight there and back. Though she never said she would do that. She may have been caught in conversation with Brenda, or maybe she decided to go for a walk or cycle along the strand. She is two decades older than him, so the journey would likely take longer. Especially the return leg, where you have more incline to deal with, and need to pedal into the strong sea wind. No longer wanting to clean, he turns the armchair back to its former position, allowing him a view of the road. He sits down and, extracting a bookmark, opens the book he started last night. He reads the same paragraph five times before closing it with a sigh, realising a moment too late that he forgot to put back the bookmark.

Rain pelts the sink window as a squall passes along the flank of the headland, racing inland. He curses. He should never have let her go to get the candles. They could have managed without them. Or, at least, he should have travelled in instead of her. Sammy could have watched her, maybe, kept her indoors. Best-case scenario now, she gets soaked; worst-case he would rather not consider, though the image still comes to mind: Helena searching out those pools on the Black Rock, watching the squall trail along the bay, walkers fleeing to the shelter of cars, dunes, and seeing her chance.

The squall passes within moments, a brightness gathering, but even that shows how the wind is picking up. It'll be a gale soon.

'Right,' he says, standing. 'Come on, Sam, we'll start walking towards her.'

Sammy rises from the floor, tail wagging at the mention of a walk. Micheál grabs his coat off the hook, pockets his gloves in case they're needed. He will meet her on the road soon enough, he tells himself, but, if not, he'll keep walking until he reaches the village. If there is still no sighting of her, he'll call in to Brenda. Ask if she has been in – a woman in her sixties with stylish red-flecked glasses who was looking to buy candles. If he has no luck with that, he can check the strand, the area where her family's old summer home used to be. Then, if she is still nowhere to be found, he will have to call Adrian Spring, get him involved.

Outside, he zips up his jacket, feels strong gusts push him down the hill and towards the gate. Sammy barks, rushing ahead, and when Micheál looks up he sees a red figure on a bike, struggling towards him.

LIV

Those nights when his parents stayed outside with a visitor. His stomach would grow more unsettled the longer they were gone. Some nights, when rainy, foggy or moonless, the cliffs were out of sight; there was no way of telling if his parents were still up there. Maybe a strong gust had knocked them over the edge, maybe the visitor was drunk or angry or not in their right mind and decided to drag his parents over the edge with them? But his parents had told him never to come up to the cliffs when they were with a visitor, so he would stay indoors. In bed, he willed himself to remain awake until they returned. When he did fall asleep, he'd often wake again with a start. He'd try and lie still for a while and listen for any sound from within the house. If all was quiet, he'd sneak down the hallway to his parents' room, put his ear to the door and wait for the murmur of voices, the sounds of them getting ready for bed. Only when they were home did he know that he would sleep.

In later years, he still startled awake. Nadine, at first, was concerned, rubbed his back, asked what was wrong. 'Just a nightmare,' he'd always reply. After a while, though, she grew frustrated. And it wasn't just the startling. It was how he couldn't sleep near the edge of the bed, would get bouts of vertigo where he felt about to fall from a great height and, in his sleep, always came towards her, clutched himself to her. It was how he would often jump at sudden loud sounds or if she appeared unexpectedly in a room behind him. 'You'd swear you had PTSD,' she said. After a particularly rough night, she even suggested going to a psychiatrist. He said maybe when things quietened down at work. At the time, he wondered what she suspected had happened in his past. Well, she knew exactly what it was now. It had been enough to drive her away. But, no, that isn't right. He had driven her away.

55

The weather worsens as the afternoon shifts into evening. Micheál spends this time preparing for the storm: making sure all the windows are shut, the pots and bike brought in – wheeled down the hallway and stashed in his bedroom – stacking spare batteries on the kitchen table beside the flashlight, the matches, and a fifty-pack of tealight candles, like the ones you'd see under the feet of a saint. Helena had handed them over with evident pride when they met at the gate. She had been caught in that squall, alright, her hair wet and dishevelled, her jacket a darker shade of red than when she'd left. He should have given her a hat at least, he'd chided himself as he wheeled the bike up the hill, Helena beside him, still in search of her breath.

Inside, she asked if she could use the shower. He retrieved

a towel from the hot press and a spare navy dressing gown that had belonged to either Áine or Saoirse. It's possible they shared it over the years. She spent a long time in the shower and re-emerged saying she wanted to take a small nap. No problem, he said. 'Let me just show you one thing before you head off.' In the far corner of the visitors' room, hidden from view from the hallway by the wardrobe, was a wooden storage chest, inside of which was a trove of clothes, a few belonging to him and his sisters, but most others simply left here by visitors over the years. 'Just throw your clothes there on the rad or in the hallway to dry, and in the meantime you can stick on something from this box of high fashion – if you want, of course.'

'That's perfect, thank you. I'll just rest for a half hour or so.'

That was four hours ago. She is still asleep, her deep breathing audible whenever he passes the room. The cycle must have really taken it out of her, he thinks, a clang of guilt in his chest.

Out the sink window, the sea seems to have more sea horses than sea. There's likely another, more appropriate name for them, but that's what his mother always called those brief, white-tipped surges. Waves crashing against the far side of Illauntannig are visible, vaulting the land. All the lights on the peninsula opposite have already been lost to the approaching storm.

He reaches to the radio on the sill; making sure the volume is low, he turns it on and switches to Radio Kerry for the six o'clock news. He hears a reiteration of the nationwide red warnings. There is a storm surge warning along the west coast, winds expected to gust as high as 160–180 km/hr. The report ends with a warning to avoid coastal areas if at all possible, and to stay inside unless absolutely necessary during the duration of the red warning. He wonders if these warnings would keep a potential visitor away, or instead entice them – better to be remembered as a storm-gazing, thrill-seeking idiot than a suicide, some might think. He'd had visitors during storms before, though not in anything as bad as this was forecast to be.

'What are they saying on the news?' Helena asks behind him.

Micheál jumps, then laughs. 'Jesus, you're up, so. I hope the radio didn't –' When he turns he sees what she has chosen from the chest: a pair of black jeans that seem a good fit for her, except for being short on the legs, and a deep-green woollen jumper, which is a perfect fit. It belonged to his mother. In fact, it had been her favourite jumper. He'd been sure that all her clothes were packed away in the attic.

Micheál forces himself to stop looking at the jumper. 'Tea?'

'That'd be lovely, yes.'

Relieved to turn away from her, he tries to compose himself as he fills the kettle. 'I was going to throw on some food as well. Are you hungry?'

'Not especially, no. But please cook away for yourself, if you are.'

'How about I put on some extra for you and if you want to eat it you can and if not you can always reheat it?'

'Sounds good,' she says.

After a dinner of chicken fillets, baked potatoes and frozen veg, of which Helena has little-to-none, they retire to the couch. He wants to ask her to change out of the jumper, though knows he cannot. He returns to the kitchen and pours himself a glass of whiskey.

'Would you like some?' he asks.

'Maybe a little,' she says. 'But could you mix it with some water, please?'

He brings over both glasses, the bottle tucked between his upper arm and chest.

'To Jerome,' he cheers once seated.

She smiles. 'To Jerome.'

Outside now the darkness is complete; the only signs of a world are the howling wind and frequent splattering of rain against the windows. Helena finishes her glass and pours herself another – no water this time. After a sip, and subsequent grimace, she begins speaking, as if the drink, or the rest, has opened something in her: 'Richard and I came down here a few times, early in our marriage. Before we were making any real money, long before we got our little place in Viareggio. He never seemed to love it, down here, certainly not as much as I did, but he didn't hate it either. The last time we came here, he was stung by a jellyfish. It wasn't even in the sea; it was on the strand, but the poor thing mustn't have been dead yet. Richard was a gentle giant of a man, never swore in his entire life. But, in that moment, in his shock, he turned the strand blue. Everyone turned to us. There was a child nearby, mustn't have been more than five or six, wild shrub of black hair on his head. He looked to his father and asked what a cunt was. It was such a small thing, of course, but it did seem to turn him fully against the place. "Jellyheigue", he began to call it, like it was something out of a T. S. Eliot story for children. He refused to go down to the strand for the rest of that trip. The next year we holidayed in Italy for the first time.'

She takes another sip of the whiskey, no grimace this time. When she looks at him, Micheál simply nods, not wanting to speak in case it stops her from offering more of her story. 'The funny thing was, though. After he got sick, it wasn't Viareggio he talked about escaping to; it was here. He wanted more than anything to come back here one final time. I couldn't understand why. It's one of the biggest regrets of my life that I never asked him. He was very sick at that point, too sick to go away on any sort of trip, so his doctor said. Not even a day trip. One evening, out of the blue, Richard asked me, "Do you think the child, whenever he hears or says the C-word, he thinks of me, hopping red-faced on the sand?" Given what we were going through, it took me a moment to realise he meant cunt, not cancer; it took me that split second to place the memory. I told him that it was likely, said he was a hard man to forget even under normal circumstances. That seemed to satisfy him.'

'He sounds like a good man,' Micheál offers.

'He was, for the most part. There aren't many around who are wholly good, but he came very close.'

She finishes her whiskey, stares out the window for a moment, then stands. 'I'm going to have another little lie-down, I think. The whiskey has gone straight to my head; I don't have the tolerance I once had.'

Another jab of guilt as Micheál thinks back to earlier, getting her to cycle in to the village. 'Of course, get all the rest you need. I'll be here if you need anything.'

'You're a good man, you know,' she says, patting his shoulder as she walks past. He can feel her touch on his shoulder long after she has gone.

LVI

He has often wondered if the visitors ever think about him. He never follows up on any of them, even in cases where he has been given phone numbers, addresses. He tells himself that he is afraid to remind them of such a dark moment in their lives. That the last thing he wants is to bring them back to their mindset when they last saw him.

He asked his mother once, 'Do they think about us?' Do they remember what we did for them?' Looking back, he knows he asked it in a selfish way, wanting praise or even gifts. They had been sitting at the kitchen table, tired and cold after a visit. He is unsure if this part of the memory is accurate, but he remembers her wearing that green woollen jumper as she leaned forward and responded: 'We don't do this for reward, Micheál. We are doing this because no one else will. And because God wants us to be here, to help them. He has chosen us.'

She never wore her religion as an armour; hers was a kind-hearted Catholicism, a gentle hand on the shoulder as opposed to a knuckle rap. But her faith was also an integral part of her drive with the visitors; in this, she had a fierce certainty. This was her fated role.

And she kept track of them in a way that he did not, with

a roster of souls, as he thought of it, written into Aisling copy books that she'd pilfer from him or one of his sisters, whoever had a spare, during the school year. She kept them tucked away in the press behind the Gleann na nGealt water, but sometimes he'd take one out, read through the list. The details varied, some bare sketches – *11/07: man, 50s, drunk* – while others gave a clearer shot of the visits:

26/10
Man (boy, really), early 20s, Aidan Dineen

Walked all the way from Tralee in the rain. Not even a coat on him. Silent for 2/3 hours up on the cliff. No response to mothering or scolding or Shane's cajoling. Very muted/withdrawn. No obvious hook when he finally started talking. Can't go on feeling like this, he said. Better to feel nothing than this. Started crying, eyes closed. Shane threw arms around his waist when clear he wasn't watching us. Dragged him back from edge. No fight from Aidan. Cried harder. Called Spring to take him to the asylum in Killarney. Agreed to pray while waiting.

The local priest, Fr Burke, often visited while Micheál and his siblings were growing up. A squat, pale man with a flattened nose, his laugh had something of the dog to it, an asthmatic bark. The good cutlery and plates were brought out, the white-and-red China teapot, the leftover biscuits and Club Orange from Christmas. The priest knew about the visitors, but Micheál wonders now if he knew that his mother used him, and later Áine, to help her save souls. Was it something she confessed to him? Would she have even seen it as something wrong? A sin?

Fr Burke visited him shortly after Nadine left. He saw his old Ford Escort, at least twenty years old, struggle towards the house, all belch and whiny rev. The priest looked much the same, standing at the front door. A touch smaller, perhaps, forehead more furrowed. Likely he just wanted to talk, maybe even help, but Micheál refused him entry. There was no faith here anymore, no soul.

Fr Burke has retired now, Brenda told him a while back. A guitar-playing cleric from Blarney called O'Connor replaced him. This new priest has never made an appearance. Perhaps Fr Burke didn't tell him what happens out here. Perhaps he thought it best that way. Steer him clear of the place of a godless man and those seeking to fall.

57

Well after midnight, Micheál lies in bed, casting about for sleep. Above his head, the bedroom window shakes with the strength of the gusts. The wind won't stop screaming. Giving up, he rises, still in his clothes and shoes, prepared to move should Helena try anything. It does seem like she has passed through the worst of it. Sammy, made anxious by the storm, had been trying to sleep at the end of his bed, but it looks like he has failed, too, as he drops to the floor and follows Micheál to the kitchen. On the way, he puts his ear to the door of the visitors' room; after a moment, heavy, rhythmic breathing reaches him. He's not sure how she can sleep through this, but is glad she has found a way.

At the entrance, he flicks the light switch. Nothing. Great, he thinks. He fumbles his way to the couch, grabbing a fist of tealight candles and the matches from the table on the way, and sits down, releasing the candles from his grip so that they create a small wax and plastic cairn atop the coffee table. This should be enough light.

He is not reading for long when the storm reaches its zenith. Micheál doubts that he's ever experienced anything like it. Maybe Storm Darwin back in 2014. These winds must be hurricane-strength. He puts down the book, listens. It sounds like something is going to take off outside, a jet or something bigger, emitting this high-pitched shriek. Sammy has retreated under the kitchen table. Part of Micheál wonders if he should join him. Another, larger part imagines what would happen were he to stand, walk to the door and, without hesitation, give himself up to the tumult.

LVIII

She didn't look like herself — that was the first thing he noticed. When had her hair gotten so thin and wispy? Her cheekbones had never been that pronounced, surely, and there was the waxiness of her face, as if this were a double prepared for display at Madame Tussauds and his real mother would appear at any moment. He almost spoke aloud — to

Áine, to the undertaker – that there had been a mistake. This was another person dressed in his mother's clothes. An imposter.

The hands gripping the rosary beads were the giveaway: those frail baby fingers, the faded scar between her thumb and forefinger from the time she was chopping carrots and movement outside the window distracted her for one slicing moment. Only a jackdaw in flight, it turned out, but the cut had required four stitches. Those hands belonged to his mother. Still, he was unable to touch them, certain, if he did, that the cold residing in them would pass into him.

There was a moderate turnout at the removal and funeral, though not to the level he expected. As neighbours and vaguely remembered people shook his and Áine's hands – Saoirse had been unable to make it back in time from Thailand; had decided since she would not make it in time not to return at all – he was forced to keep down a rising fury. After all she had done for this community, after all she had put him and his sisters through, for the sake of strangers, this was the send-off she got? No more than thirty-odd souls standing awkwardly in a graveyard on a grey day, even those present seeming less focused on acknowledging her than on having their umbrellas at the ready, should the sky fall.

59

The candlelight is too weak to read. A strain in his eyes, Micheál takes his phone from his pocket – maybe he can prop the phone up against a stack of other books, angle it so that the light shines directly on the open page. He clicks the on button, notices the date, and a realisation settles on him: 8 March. It had been his father's anniversary yesterday, and he'd forgotten all about it. He sits still a moment, listening to the storm, the roof remaining on the point of lifting right off.

Áine would normally ring him on the day – neither had an interest in arranging an anniversary Mass, but still, in previous years, he'd always remembered it in advance. Braced for it, in a way. Suitable weather at least, he thinks.

He would normally expect his thoughts to turn to his father, but this year he finds himself thinking of his mother. He is the same age now as his mother had been when it happened – Jesus. The loss. Needing time and space, to figure out what to do with all the love she had for him. What he still fails to understand is why she decided to give it to the visitors, rather than her children. Because that is where she put it – most of it, anyway.

Sometimes, he wonders if she thought she was doing what his father wanted. When Micheál tries to picture his father, he sees him sitting on the wicker chair, still dressed from his day of teaching, though the tie has been discarded, the top buttons of his crisp shirt opened. He remembers a kind man, a patient man, who showed him how to hurl and introduced him, with genuine excitement, to Tolkien and C. S. Lewis. But he has so few concrete memories of his father, would likely have trouble picturing his face were it not for old photographs. When he recalls his youth now, so much of it revolves around the visitors or memories associated with them. That's where the colour lies, the detail. As if they have drawn the clarity from other aspects of his past, leaving them grey, sketchy, indistinct. Even the memory of his father he's returned to most these past few years has visitors wrapped up in it.

LX

Two or maybe three summers before his father died the family holidayed for a long weekend in Lahinch. They stayed in a caravan owned by Uncle Mikey. The weekend was spent on and near the beach, acting just like the families they often saw at that time of year in Ballyheigue. They built sand castles, carved tennis courts in the sand, regularly sprinted to the sea, the water extra cold against bodies that had taken in the sun's glare all day. At one point, his father suggested a trip to the nearby Cliffs of Moher, 'just to see our competition', as he put it, but his mother shook her head. 'No cliffs this weekend.'

The furthest excursion they took from the shore was to go to the circus, a big tent having been erected in the town park at nearby Ennistymon. It was the only time in his life that Micheál went to the circus. He remembers the smell of dung and straw outside the big top, the scent of the pink swirl of candy floss inside. It had all seemed so exotic: the lion tamer, acrobats, the sword-swallower and elephants. At the interval, his father paid for Áine and Saoirse to ride a camel around the ring. He offered Micheál a go, too, but he shook his head, considered himself too old for such a thing. Saoirse cried when she was taken off the camel, wanting another go.

When they got back to the caravan, their father sat on the block steps outside with a map spread across his knees – looking for a place to explore the following day, he said. Micheál heard his mother say, 'I'm sure the kids would rather just stay by the beach.' His father grumbled, 'I just think it'd be better to get a head start – we can always stop at the beach in Ballybunion on the way back.' Later, as his parents prepared dinner, and Micheál sat on the couch with his Gameboy, Áine and Saoirse began squabbling in their room. He forgets what it was over now, but knows that it ended with a shattering. His father stormed down the narrow galley-kitchen to the bedroom, saw on the floor the remains of a wood-based, crystal clock that had been sitting on the bedside table.

Never before nor after did he see his father as angry, his voice so loud that Micheál – and his mother, judging from her anxious glances out the window – was sure that those in the neighbouring caravans could hear every word. After your uncle is kind enough to let us borrow the caravan. Do you have any idea? How ungrateful. Disrespectful.

Straight after dinner, they were told to pack and load everything into the car. A day early, the holiday was over. They just made the last ferry to Tarbert, the sun blushing the Shannon as they crossed. It was pitch dark by the time they arrived at Kerry Head.

He has often looked back at that, seeing it for what it was: an overreaction. But recently, he also thinks about what Áine once told him. How, in the years when he was away and she helped with the visitors, their mother once confided that she had wanted to sell the land after her own mother died. She had changed her mind about them living out here. It was our father who convinced her to stay, Áine said. He was the one who told her that they had important work to do here. That they could not shirk their responsibility.

At the time, Micheál refused to believe it, but now his mind returns to his father, red-faced in the caravan, slapping his hand against the wheel of the car when they were stuck behind a tractor on those narrow Clare country roads, desperate to make the final ferry.

61

The storm eases throughout the morning. By lunchtime, the red warning has lifted for this part of the country. Micheál has already been outside a number of times to check and recheck the house; miraculously, no damage is visible. Across the road, the Spillanes' hayshed has lost a section of its tin roof, the sheet sticking out of a ditch further east on his land.

The radio, running on batteries, offers a fresh litany of local damage at the top of every hour: the coastal walkway at Fenit uprooted, the roof torn off the gym of the Mercy Mounthawk secondary school in Tralee, a caravan site flooded down in Caherdaniel, many of the caravans washed out to sea. There are reports of a large number of fallen trees in the national park in Killarney. Numerous roads throughout the county are impassable. The Rossbeigh spit is also said to be damaged, maybe even cut through at one point, leaving houses and farmland in Cromane at risk of flooding.

'The county took a battering,' Micheál says after listening to the latest round of news.

'It certainly seems so,' Helena responds. She sits opposite him at the kitchen table, both of them drinking lukewarm tea from the flask that Micheál had filled before the power cut out. Helena had stayed in her room for the worst of the storm, only venturing out as it eased. She is still wearing his mother's jumper.

He glances outside, notes the light sky. He feels a restlessness in him. He hasn't been out for a walk in a couple of days, and, if he's honest with himself, he wants to have a look along the headland, see if there's any other damage, hear any stories, if he were to bump into neighbours.

'Do you fancy a walk?' he asks.

Sammy's head rises from his paws, tail brushing the floor.

'I would, actually, yes,' Helena responds.

They both wrap up, Micheál giving her a spare fleece, gloves and Man Utd wool hat, all of which are too big for her, but at least they'll keep her warm.

Outside, the bay is a darker, earthier hue than normal, like it has taken into it some of the land. Closer to shore, waves continue to crash over the sliver of rock that is Illaunnabarnagh. The sea will be wild for days yet, he knows, aftershocks of the storm. There'll be a parade of surfers out along the strand in the coming week.

As Micheál and Helena start towards the gate, Sammy's nose lifts into the air and, without warning, he bolts towards the cliff. Micheál scans the field, the clifftop. There are no visitors in sight. 'Sammy,' he calls, but the dog continues on, rushing in among the long grass and wildflowers. The flap of a vibrant wing. Sammy barks, moves closer. The creature hidden in the undergrowth gives another half-hearted flap and is still.

'Sammy!' Micheál shouts, rushing towards him. 'Get back.'

The dog retreats a few steps, whining.

Micheál moves closer, sees in the long grass a bird: black crown, though with shades of dark green, pointed yellow bill and a long elegant neck striped white and chestnut.

'It's unusual looking, isn't it?' Helena says behind him. 'What type of bird is it, do you think?'

'I'm not sure,' he says.

'What's wrong with it?'

'Looks exhausted,' he says. 'And there may be some damage to its wing.' He moves closer. The bird barely moves, all its remaining strength likely used in trying to get away from Sammy. It stares at him as he touches it on the neck, the chest, then retreats. Cold to the touch, as he'd suspected. 'Here, I need you to do a few things for me, if that's okay?'

'Of course.'

'First off, can you take Sammy inside and lock him in – he'll have the bird scared to death if he stays out here. When you're inside, I need you to get a few things and bring them out to me. I'll need a towel, a big towel – you can get one in the hot press. Get me gloves, too; they're up on the sideboard. And a cardboard box – there are a few up in the attic. There's one from the old TV, you'll see Mitsubishi on the side. It's filled with clothes or photo albums or something like that now, but just dump them out and bring it to me. Oh, but before you do, get a knife and make tiny holes on each side of the box.' Helena frowns. 'For ventilation,' he explains. 'And line the bottom with some newspaper; there should be some old editions under the coffee table.'

With Helena and Sammy gone, Micheál crouches in the long grass, near the bird but not close enough that it feels threatened. The long bill and neck suggest a type of crane or heron, though it's not a native species, of that he's sure. Much smaller than any of the Irish varieties. The storm must have blown the poor thing off course. But just how far had it strayed?

Sooner than expected, Helena returns. Micheál puts on the gloves, readies the towel. He should be wearing protective glasses, too – the bird's beak looks particularly sharp – but he will just have to be careful. He gives the container a final check – it is open and ready, each side looking like it'd been sprayed with a shotgun – and moves towards the bird.

The bird offers little resistance. As he lies the towel over it, the only visible movement is the rapid fluttering of its chest. As delicately as he can, Micheál wraps the bird in the towel, lifts it and carries it to the container. Once in the box, he removes the towel, newspaper crinkling as he does. Its head moves slightly, beak finding cardboard, but other than that it is still as he closes the box, putting the towel over it to keep the lid in place. He has a strong urge to talk to the bird, to try to soothe it, but he'd read somewhere that you shouldn't do that; if anything, it can panic them further.

Once inside, Sammy begins barking and scurrying around the kitchen table. 'Could you put him outside?' he asks Helena. As she drags Sammy out, with difficulty, he fills a little see-through Tupperware container with water and places it into the box beside the bird's head. Its eye fixes on him, chest beating faster still.

Lid back on, he gets a blanket and places it over the box; it's long enough, unlike the towel, to cover the entire container. This should further darken the inside of the box, which will in turn reduce its stress. It might even get some sleep.

'How is it?' Helena asks once back inside.

'Hard to say. We'll see if it takes any water, I guess.'

He goes to his laptop, planning to search for what type of bird it is, but the power is still out. No Internet. His phone might have some data left. He takes it from his jeans pocket, clicks on the search engine. He types in its identifiers. A couple of different pictures come up, one of which confirms the bird as a least bittern.

He shows the picture and information to Helena.

'It came a long way, didn't it?'

'It must have been an odyssey, alright,' he agrees.

'What now?' she asks.

'I better call Trish.'

The phone rings for at least two minutes before he gets an answer. 'Hello?' Trisha Dennehy shouts. She must be in her car, the sound of gravelly movement and pop country music in the background. A slender, blonde woman in her late thirties, Trish had taken over the veterinary practice in Ardfert from her father around the same time that Micheál moved back to the area. Brenda told him once how many of the older farmers expected her to fail. Some had even put money on it, she said, but Trish thrived; many of those former sceptics now worship the ground on which she walks. As Brenda put it, the only one making money out of those old farmers now was Trish herself.

'Trish, it's Micheál Burns, you know out on Kerry Head?'

'Everything okay with Sammy?' she asks, getting straight to the point. He'd only go to her once or twice a year with the dog, but she has no trouble remembering his name.

'No, no, the dog is fine. It's just I've found a bird on my land – a type of small American heron called a least bittern, if you can believe it. The storm must have blown it over here all the way from the States. I'd have to check to be certain, but I'm not sure if there's ever been one sighted here.'

The music stops on the other side of the line. 'Right. Where is it now?'

'Well, we found it out in the field. It didn't have the strength to move, it was cold to the touch, so I felt the best thing to do was capture it and bring it in somewhere warm,' he says, for the first time thinking that maybe he'd done the wrong thing. Should he have left it outside? Should he have waited longer before capturing it, giving it more of a chance to recover by itself? 'It's inside now in a cardboard box, with the lid on. There are holes on the sides for ventilation, it has enough space to move around, and I've put water inside.'

'Right, has it taken any of the water?'

'I haven't checked yet; we've only just brought it inside.'

'Well, check that when you get off the phone. It's a heron, you say. Do you have any fish in the house? Preferably something like sprat or herring?'

He hurries to the fridge, opens it. 'I've some salmon darnes left, a couple of pieces of cod.'

'The salmon would be better. Break it into small chunks – make sure to get rid of any bones – and put them into its water bowl. Then just keep an eye on it and see if it's taking any of the water or the fish. I'm in Abbeyfeale right now – my dad caught me to do an errand for him – but I'll be there as soon as I can.'

After she hangs up, Micheál turns to Helena. 'Help is on the way.'

She lets out a sigh. 'Good.'

LXII

After his sisters had gone from the headland, Micheál stopped travelling home altogether. He rang less, too. He saw his mother just once a year, for lunch, on the Sunday nearest the anniversary of his father's death. It was a tradition that had started in his first year in college.

The venue was the same every year. They met in Abbeyfeale, exactly halfway between Kerry Head and Limerick, as if it were a parley as opposed to a meeting between mother and son. McCourt's Tavern was a pub-restaurant designed solely for the many – primarily American – tourists who passed through. It even had a thatched roof, which drew the Yanks like flies to light. Or shit. Still, his mother liked their roast chicken. Only one year did she alter this arrangement, postponing it by a week, as she had a visitor staying with her at the time. 'A poor boy from out near Lixnaw,' she explained over the phone. 'The black moods just take him sometimes, he says. I've told him he's welcome to stay here till the mood has passed.'

That final Sunday, she arrived before him. He saw her sitting at a table by one of the front windows, still dressed in her Mass outfit: black pants, a floral shirt that reminded him of the wildflowers around their home, a slim gold necklace that he knew had been a birthday present from his father. Her hair was different, he noticed, as he got closer: shorter, fringed, the grey (she had stopped dyeing it after his father's death) now stranded white. He could have said something, complimented it, but he didn't, perhaps still frustrated at having to inch through the typical bottleneck of traffic in Adare, or set aside his lesson prep for the week ahead to come to this annual farce of a get-together. Or maybe it was a resentment born of the feeling that always blossomed in him when he saw her – the fear that at any moment she would order him to get his boots and coat, the flashlight, and summon him to follow her.

She half-stood, almost crouched, when she saw him approach, but was sitting again by the time he reached the table, as if realising it better not to try for a hug or kiss. The conversation began with the usual small talk: the drive (Adare was Adare; she chanced the back roads through Duagh after hearing about roadworks outside Castleisland); the weather ('filthy' down on Kerry Head, no different in Limerick); what they would order (he went with his usual steak and chips, though she departed from her typical roast chicken, instead ordering the salmon with sauce on the side. 'Easier on the stomach,' she said).

After the orders were taken, an awkward silence lingered.

In that space were all the things they had agreed not to discuss: the visitors, Saoirse's never coming home, the visitors, his never coming home, the visitors.

'Have you gone for your check-up?'

'Last month. Everything's fine. I told you that already.'

She gave him a level look. 'Yes, but it's harder to tell if you're lying on the phone.'

'What? I've lied to you loads over the years.'

'Yes, but I could always tell.'

'Well, I'm not lying. About the check-up.'

'I can see that.'

Micheál sighed.

With a sudden grunt, his mother leaned down towards her handbag on the shamrock-patterned carpet, pulled out a 350 ml bottle with a half-torn Ballygowan sticker around it, and tried to pass it to him furtively under the table, as if this were a drug deal. 'Should keep you going awhile; make sure to give some to Nadine too.' He took the bottle and, looking around, quickly put it into the inner pocket of his jacket, which was hanging off the back of his chair. He didn't want the staff to think he distrusted their water, had brought his own. Every year she did this, brought him a bottle of Gleann na nGealt water. He always dumped it down the sink as soon as he was back at the apartment. After Áine's last visit home to Kerry Head, she told him how she'd noticed extra containers of the stuff, some as big as ten litres, stashed in the cupboard by the freezer. His mother had to be visiting the valley more than once a year to have hoarded that much well water. He wondered how much of it she was drinking a day.

It was mid-meal when he first noticed the pull in her: a twitchiness in her hands, repeated glances at her watch, out the window towards her car, a sudden rush to her eating. She called for the bill before she'd even finished. No time for dessert. She had to get back. Expected as it was, it still stung, seeing the eagerness in her to be away. It hurt too, as he was aware that, for all the resentment and anxiety that travelled with him to those meetings, so too was there a hope that, this time, there might be a sighting of doubt, regret, maybe even contrition. There never was. The only thing that differed that final meeting was her switch from chicken to salmon.

63

The power comes back on in the late afternoon, announced by the low hum of the fridge and the turning on of the light above the kitchen table. Not that it matters; it is much too late to save most of the food in the fridge and freezer. Micheál fills the kettle and takes it down to his room, where he boils it, far enough away that the sound shouldn't unsettle the heron. When he returns to the kitchen, he brings with him two cups of tea.

'Thanks,' Helena says as he hands her a cup and sits beside her on the couch. She has placed a jug of lukewarm milk and the bowl of sugar on the coffee table. He puts a splash of the milk into his tea. A black station wagon appears on the road, continues on past the gate.

'She's taking her time,' Helena says.

'She has a fair way to come. She was over in Limerick on business.'

Though staring ahead, most of Micheál's attention is fixed on the box behind, alert for any sound or rustling. He wants to avoid opening the lid too often. When he last checked he saw that the level of the water in the Tupperware container was down, and the bird felt warmer, but the salmon remained untouched.

Helena holds the cup in both her hands, though she has yet to drink from it. 'It's a terrible feeling, this – the helplessness of waiting for help to arrive.'

Micheál grunts, not wanting to disagree with her.

'I used to get it a lot, with Richard, towards the end. Particularly once he'd moved into the hospice. The discomfort, the outright pain. It took everything I had to see him through it, to be with him to the end.' She pauses. 'And then to hear that I had a similar journey ahead of me, but I'd have to do it without him. It was too much, really; it just felt like too much.'

'Helena –'

'We were always too alike for our own good, Richard and I.'

Micheál struggles for words, finds himself departing from his mother's script. 'I could help, I could do something.'

'You've done more than enough. Really. Besides, I wasn't completely honest with you before. I do have some family left. My sister, Cathy. I hate the idea of burdening her, but I know that she'll be there for me if I need it. I would like to spend a few more days here, though, before I go back. If that's okay with you?'

'Of course.' He smiles. 'You can stay as long as you'd like.'

Movement out the window draws their gaze: a Land Rover down at the gate.

'I think they call that perfect timing, don't they?' Helena says.

Trish enters, flustered, her blond hair tied back in a pony-tail. Her broad shoulders hint at her stature as a hardy centre back on the Clanmaurice camogie team. 'Sorry for the delay; I took the back roads through Abbeydorney to save time, but there was a tree down, so I'd to double back.' She nods towards Helena, who responds in kind, then looks at the box on the kitchen table and lowers her voice. 'How's it doing?'

'Seems to be taking some water, alright, but no food. Feels warmer than before, too. Still exhausted, though. Very little movement.'

She nods and takes clear plastic gloves from her pocket as she moves towards the box. The blanket is slid off, lid lifted. She leans over, squints inside. A gloved hand reaches down, feels around. A second hand lowers down, and she moves the bird, with care, on to its other side. It offers no resistance. She leans closer, her head almost in the box, then retreats. The lid is placed back on, as is the blanket.

'Okay, I'm going to need to take it into the clinic with me. I think you're right about the wing, Mick, but its biggest problem is that we need to get it eating again. And I'll need to put it on rehydration fluid straight away, if it's to have any chance.'

'Is there any more I can do?' Micheál asks.

'You've done as much as you can.'

He helps her put the container in the back seat of her Land

Rover. She puts the seatbelt around it to stop it from sliding around.

'I'll call you with updates, okay?'

'Okay, thanks.'

Back inside, Trish's rear red lights gone from view, a sudden wave of exhaustion forces him on to the nearest chair. He feels nearly faint with the tiredness. Or maybe he just feels faint. Helena appears beside him. 'You look spent. Will I cook us something? I could cook some of the meat in the freezer; it's just going to go to waste otherwise.'

The thought of food makes him nauseous. 'No, no, I couldn't eat right now.'

She kneels beside him. 'You need to sleep,' she says. 'You know what I thought when I saw you up on the cliff – that man looks in desperate need of a good night's rest. You look more ill than I do. Honestly, that's the first thought I had seeing that face of yours.'

His attempt at a laugh is more of a deep sigh. 'I sleep, I get some sleep.'

'I bet you can't remember the last time you got a decent night's sleep.'

Micheál finds himself standing and being led down the hallway by Helena. In his bedroom, he wavers as Helena moves aside the quilt and directs him to lie down. At this stage, he has stopped resisting. He lies on the bed, his legs hanging off the side. He's not sure he has ever felt this tired. It weighs on him like the heavier gravity of a different planet.

Helena removes one boot, then the other. He feels like a child. She lifts his legs on to the mattress, pulls the quilt over him. He wants to reach a hand out, touch the deep-green of her jumper, but his hands are under the quilt, and he hasn't the strength to break them out.

She sits on the side of the bed. 'Look, your phone is in the kitchen. I'll wake you if the vet calls, okay? And I'll keep an eye out tonight. I'll stay up – I've already had so much sleep this last couple of days – so if anyone shows up, or anything odd happens, I'll come and get you straight away.'

'I'm probably not going to sleep, anyway,' he mumbles, eyes closed.

'Well, just give it a go,' she says.

When she rises, Micheál almost asks her to stay, to remain by his side for a while, but she is out in the hallway before he opens his mouth, and the moment passes. As she closes the door, the darkness comes in fast.

LXIV

'Sleep, my Superman. Sleep.' And so he did.

65

Micheál wakes to daylight and an immediate sense of absence. Even before he rises, he is certain that she is gone. As he walks down the hallway, Sammy's head appears in the kitchen, watching him with what he sees as a meek look. The visitors' room is empty, bed made. In the kitchen, Sammy's water bowl and food bowl have been filled, likely so he wouldn't come and wake Micheál too early.

Something deep and raw rising in him, he scours the kitchen for a note. Nothing. No, wait – on the coffee table. His breath catches as he reads.

Sorry to leave without saying goodbye. Thought it easiest. Just wanted you to get a good night's sleep.
Thank you for everything. Will go to sister's now to begin fight.
H x

He drops the note on the kitchen table and picks up his phone, which has three missed calls, one voicemail. Outside, there is no visible trail through the field, no sign of movement up on the cliffs. In the other direction, the gate is closed. Moving closer to the field, searching for even the faint outline of a trail, he wonders, as he had the night before, if there really is a sister.

Standing amid the wildflowers, he clicks on the voicemail, brings the phone to his ear.

Trish's sombre voice. Sorry. Came in this morning. Dead. Poor thing had just travelled too far.

PART FOUR

66

Micheál lies on the couch, watching Homer Simpson strangle his son. Beyond the TV, the evening sun has cast the headland in a yellow-golden light that, after six or seven or eight episodes, looks similar to the skin of most Springfieldians. It adds a sense of unreality to the land.

A crick forming in his neck, he shifts the doubled-over pillow behind his head. As he manoeuvres, the quilt half-covering his bare feet falls to the floor, landing on a napping Sammy. The dog's head pokes out from under the quilt and he lets out a snort.

'Sorry.'

Micheál rises from the couch, with considerable effort, at the end of the episode. Everything takes considerable effort now. The heaviness that had loomed after Brenda's party was held off during Helena's stay, but since Trish took the heron away it has settled over him, each day weighing him down a little more. He is still stuck on that different, denser planet. He has avoided climbing to the attic, has avoided opening his notebook for the ships or birds. Most of his time is now spent on the couch.

At the fridge, he considers cooking a proper meal – meat,

veg, two or three spuds – but instead takes out the butter and puts another two slices of white bread into the toaster. He reboils the kettle, enough left in it for one more cup. There are no clean plates, but he unearths a side plate from the overfilled sink – it has only been used for toast, crumbs stuck to it and a stained dollop of leftover butter.

Putting the toast and tea on the coffee table, he sees a missed call on his phone: 066. Tralee number. It must be that woman from the *Kerry's Eye* again. Word about the heron had spread. It turned out that it had been the first-ever sighting of the bird in Ireland, or mainland Europe; in fact, it was only the eighth-ever sighting in the Western Palaearctic. According to Trisha, the Natural History Museum in Dublin is looking to preserve it in its vaults. The woman at the newspaper – he forgets her name – has rung a number of times, looking to set up an interview. She wants to call out to the house, maybe bring a photographer. It is the last thing he needs right now.

He lies back on the couch, cup of tea in hand, and considers trying Netflix, see if anything new has been released. He still uses Áine's password, as she never told him to stop: a minor – and admittedly petty – act of defiance. In the end, he isn't bothered enough to reach for the laptop, go through the rigmarole of setting it up. Another episode of *The Simpsons* begins on the TV. Within ten seconds he recognises the episode, can see along the entire length of the story. There is something comforting in that. Or deadening, at least. Over the years, he has put together a routine that has kept the past more or less at bay – it was always there under the surface, sure, but since the ultimatum, and particularly since Brenda's party, it has all become untethered in his mind, set to drift. None of the memories are new. He keeps returning to the same ones, sharpening them to a fine point.

LXVII

After dinner, Micheál plugged the sink, squirted Fairy Liquid across the ware. Outside, the sea was lost from sight in the darkness, though a strong south-westerly brought the clear, weighted sound of it to him, even through the shut window.

As the sink filled with water, he turned and found Nadine staring at the table, running her hand across the paisley-patterned tablecloth. After a moment, as if having waited for him to turn, she pulled the cloth from the table with a quick, magician-like flourish.

He frowned at her.

'Look! It's so much nicer without the tablecloth, right?' she said.

His gaze fell to the now-exposed wood, a crevice of a chip at one edge and a swirling dark mark near its centre, like an eye or a black hole. He brought a palm to it, felt along its surface. There was a roughness to the table that he liked, a naturalness, as if it had grown from the earth in that exact shape. Not been cut or moulded, simply formed.

'It is, yeah.'

'And, you know, now that I've had a few days here, I can see there are a lot of things we can do – just small things, mind – that could make the house feel more like our own place. Like maybe get some new curtains for the bedroom, put up a painting or a couple of framed photos – maybe take down Our Lord and Saviour over there,' she said, nodding towards the bulb-hearted Jesus.

A sharp tug against the idea in his stomach. It must have shown in his face, as she added, 'Well, look, just think about it, anyway. It could be nice to freshen the place up a bit.'

'It's just that we're not going to be here for long, really, and –'

'Right,' she said, enthusiasm now gone from her voice.

'Look, I'll think about it. Just go chill out on the couch there; I'll do the ware,' he said, gesturing to the nearly over-flowing sink.

He washed the dishes, left them to dry on the rack. When he walked over to Nadine, he found her glaring at the laptop resting on her thighs. She'd spread herself across the couch in such a way that no room remained for him.

'What are you watching?' he asked.

'*Breaking Bad.*'

'Oh, I thought we were going to watch it together?'

'We were. This is how I'm punishing you for not agreeing to get new curtains.' She said it as if she were joking, though there was an edge to her words, and he remembered his mother saying once: *There's nothing as serious as a half-joke.*

He tried to peer at her screen; the angle didn't allow for a proper view. 'Can't imagine the dad from *Malcolm in the Middle* being a good dramatic actor.'

'Well, I've only watched like ten minutes, but so far he's been good.'

'Could you move over?'

She sighed, but did move. As soon as he was sitting beside her – he could see Malcolm's dad on screen, with a thick moustache and glasses, washing a sports car that didn't look like it belonged to him – she started in on it again: 'I just don't understand why you won't at least let me take down bulby Jesus. He gives me the creeps.'

He hit the spacebar on her laptop, paused the show. 'Look, yeah, okay, maybe some new curtains would be nice in the bedroom,' he said.

'You think?'

He made himself smile. 'Yeah.'

Nadine manoeuvred closer to him, rested her head against his shoulder. 'It would be nice, you know. This place would just feel more like ours, even if we do end up only being here for a little while.'

They both returned their attention to the screen. Malcolm's dad was washing the car of one of his students, it turned out. Micheál once again thanked the educational gods that he had not decided to teach at secondary level. Primary-aged children could be difficult, of course, but there was none of the open revolt and mockery of teenagers.

A loud sound outside. Micheál jolted, displacing Nadine from his shoulder. Another tug in his stomach, pulling something loose.

'What was that?' Nadine asked.

'It sounded like the bin falling over,' he said, standing. 'I'll just go check on it.' Nadine motioned to pause the show. 'No, no, keep watching it; I'll only be a minute.'

Micheál put on his jacket, stuck bare feet into heavy boots. When sure she was absorbed in the show, he walked to the press under the sink, reached to the back corner for the flash-light. It had sounded like the bin. That it was just the wind. But still. He needed to check. To make sure. God, if it was a visitor – but no, it wouldn't be.

At least it wasn't raining. Struggling against the gale, he rounded the side of the house, where he'd moved the bins earlier in the day to avoid the worst of the forecasted storm. The security light only covered the other side of the house, so he turned on the flashlight. There. The refuse bin had tipped over. As he moved closer, he felt the sudden lessening of the wind: it was too sheltered here, surely, for it to have been at fault. But if someone had been running past?

Closer now, he saw that one of the black bags was torn, its innards scattered across the ground. He turned and walked along the length of the house, to the point where the gale returned and pushed him back a step. He angled the flash-light, swept the field. Nothing on the first sweep, but then. About halfway up towards the cliff.

Two eyes. White, almost golden in colour. Shining close to the ground, he thought – though it was difficult to say from this distance. His breath stilled as he held the light to them. Then a glitch or a rippling in the surrounding dark and the eyes were gone.

Inside, Nadine watched as he stripped off his layers, the flashlight hidden in the inner pocket of his jacket. She likely took his shaking as being from the cold. 'What was it?' she asked.

And he almost told her everything then. He really al-most did.

'Just the bin,' he said. 'Like I thought.'

For a long time after he sat down, those eyes remained before him, piercing, unblinking. Judging.

68

Sammy bounds down towards the gate, nose diving to gravel, earth, finding scents of things long gone. Walking down the hill, Micheál wonders how far back a dog's nose can travel in time: minutes, hours, days? Why not months, years? Bury that nose deep enough in the dirt and maybe he comes across soldier, famine sufferer, Viking.

Once out on the road, they travel northwards. Near the turn-off for the fort, Sammy makes for the roadside ditch and a bird darts out, screeching as it flees. Micheál finds no desire in him to follow its flight, try to ascertain its type. Taking Sammy on his daily walk means mustering all of the energy he has left. At home, he lies on the couch. He still has to finish the last batch of books he borrowed from the mobile library, all of which are now long overdue. Every time he lifts one up he can only read a paragraph or two before zoning out.

As he threads over craggy rock and fern, Sammy already at the fort, Micheál spots rain clouds off Loop Head. It is hard to tell with the swirling wind in what direction the clouds are moving. Between him and the rain clouds, a cargo ship is leaving the Shannon Estuary, a far busier channel for boats than Tralee Bay. Safer, too. He'd heard on Radio Kerry how a seventeenth- or eighteenth-century shipwreck had been exposed on the Ballyheigue strand by Storm Jerome. Enough of the wreck has been exhumed to know that it was a three-mast ship. There have been suggestions that it could be the *Golden Lion*, the ship involved in the Danish Silver Robbery – so named, he has since learnt, as it was a Danish-owned ship that had set sail from Copenhagen with a cargo of silver bullion, not gold. Not all sources are reliable, it turns out. Now at least the name made sense. Part of him wants to go see the ship, to touch the heavy, sea-blackened wood, but then he thinks of bumping into Brenda in the village or on the strand. He hasn't the energy for any of it.

At the fort, he rests on the remains of a wall. Sammy scurries about, nose to earth. The cargo ship has left the estuary now, travelling into open sea. For a moment, he imagines Helena on the ship, stowing away below deck, setting out for new land, a new life. He has found his thoughts returning to her, in the way they rarely do with visitors. He should have stayed awake. He should have made her talk more about Richard, her illness. After all, why would she say she wanted to stay a few more days and then leave without warning? How would she even have got home? He'd seen no sign of keys or a wallet, no transport. Where even was home for her? Somewhere in Dublin, he supposes, but that hardly narrows it down. She never gave a surname, and there is no proof that the name Helena is real. There is no easy way of tracing her; he just has to take what she said in that note on faith. Or accept that the uncertainty will always gnaw away at him. Another thing he fucked up. He should keep a notebook of fuck-ups instead of birds and ships, if he could find one big enough.

LXIX

After finding Nadine among the wildflowers, he helped her to her feet, led her inside. She was trembling as he set her down at the kitchen table, though the afternoon was mild. He rushed to the bedroom, carried the quilt in a twisted bundle in his arms back to the kitchen, and wrapped it around her. She hardly acknowledged this, instead staring into the empty fireplace.

What to do next? He looked around, rubbed at his chest, though he knew it would do nothing to ease the tightness building inside. The press beside the fridge. Yes. He opened it, snatched the half-empty bottle of whiskey from the top shelf, where one has always resided, next to where his mother had kept the Gleann na nGealt water, which he'd poured down the sink when they arrived. He took her favourite cup from the other press, poured the whiskey into it. A double, at least.

'Drink that,' he said, sitting beside her. 'Slowly, mind.'

'I shouldn't,' she said.

'A sip won't matter.'

She sipped, winced, sipped again.

'Sometimes they're too far gone to help,' he muttered.

'What?'

'We can only do our best, d'you know?'

She squinted at him, as if coming out of a dream. 'Micheál, what are you talking about?'

He sighed, met her uncertain gaze. 'I thought maybe they'd stopped coming.'

'Who?'

Hurt and a sense of betrayal grew across her face as he spoke, but he made himself watch all of it, as he told her everything that there was to tell.

70

Another letter arrives from Áine's solicitor. This one he leaves unopened.

LXXI

The A&E was quiet at that time of night. One lad, the punch of drink off him felt from the entrance, held a bloodied tea towel to the back of his head; a pale, elderly woman sat a few rows behind him with a relative or carer, her arm held up by a makeshift sling, both women wearing baggy coats over pyjamas, dressing gowns.

A middle-aged, bespectacled nurse, upon seeing Nadine, the state she was in, came out from behind the reception. 'Get a wheelchair, John,' she ordered a nearby red-haired porter. He rushed into a back room, returned with the chair, one of the wheels squeaking on the floor. Nadine groaned as she sat into it. She was turned towards Micheál but did not look up at him.

'Take her down to Dr Hayes. Immediately, please.'

The porter nodded, started to race her down the hallway.

Micheál made to follow, but the nurse grabbed his arm. A finger pointed out the entrance, the car parked askew across the ambulance bay. 'You need to move that first,' she said.

'But –'

'The quicker you get it done, the quicker you get back to her.'

He sighed, ran outside. Both car doors were still open, hers particularly wide from when she'd struggled to rise out of the car. He closed her door, sat into the driver's side, and started the engine. Nearing the entrance to the car park, he saw the barrier gate. Shit. You had to pay to use the car park, didn't you? In his rush, he'd left his wallet at home. He stopped, reversed around to the front of the hospital, but away from the ambulance bay. Parked on double yellow lines – no one would clamp him at three in the morning, right? – by a bed of daffodils and an empty bench with a plaque on it.

Against his will, almost, his gaze dropped from the bench to the ruin of the front passenger seat. For a moment, he had an urge to put his hand to it, smear it across his face. He had a sense of needing to be marked somehow. But then he thought of Nadine, alone inside the hospital, and he was out of the car, running. It was only by the entrance to the A&E that he wondered if he'd locked the car. It doesn't matter, he thought. They could take it for all he cared. If anything, he should have left the key in the ignition. Better to never see that seat again.

72

He uses a new notebook, the last in that pack. Throughout the day, he writes what he watches:

The Big Bang Theory, Season 1, eps 1–11
Brooklyn Nine-Nine, Season 4, eps 18–22 / Season 5, eps 1–6
The Pineapple Express
Only Fools and Horses, six eps (need to Google episode nos.)

LXXIII

The morning after Nadine left, he started awake, hung-over. The first thing he noticed, apart from the splitting headache: how big the bed seemed now. All that empty space.

74

Brooklyn Nine-Nine, Season 5, eps. 1–18
The Jerk & *The Man with Two Brains*
BoJack Horseman, Season 1 & 2

LXXV

After she left, he found himself thinking about the days and weeks after her knee injury. How needed he felt. Before that, the rowing had come before everything, and he was fine with that single-mindedness, even if he sometimes felt like a bit of an afterthought. But suddenly the balance shifted. She depended upon him in a way she hadn't before. To bring her food, make sure she took her medication, comfort her. It's not that he was happy she got injured. He had just felt her drifting away from him, and the injury brought her back.

Even the proposal – at the time, he told himself it was done because he loved her, of course, but also as a way of taking her mind off the injury, dragging her out of the black pit into which she had sunk. But, looking back, he couldn't help wondering: did a part of him see this as an opportunity? To trap her at a low moment. To tie her to him.

76

BoJack Horseman, Season 3 & Season 4, eps 1–6

By evening, he has to stop watching the show. So funny. But too sad, too true. Part of Micheál wants desperately to know if the horseman redeems himself, fixes himself. More of him is afraid of the answer.

LXXVII

She gave no warning: no phone call, text, email. She just appeared at the door one afternoon, in black jeans, matching runners and a blue hiking fleece. Behind her, a blood-red Mini was parked on the plateau, and the bay was a frazzled churn of aquamarine and steel grey, after a night of high winds.

'Can I come in?' That old look of steady determination, the one she used to wear before a race.

'Of course,' he croaked, moving back, hoping she avoided getting a whiff of him. Both he and the house were a tip. When he'd imagined seeing Nadine again, and he often did, it was somewhere far from here, and he was showered and shaved, and had put in a month's worth of sit-ups and push-ups.

Inside, Sammy approached her, unusually skittish, though his tail moved in a frenzied manner. She leaned down, rubbed his head, along his flank. 'You've replaced me well, I see,' she said, reaching for humour to relieve tension. Just as she used to do.

'You never ordered me around as much.'

She laughed her honk of a laugh. The sound was a thump to his chest, the memories stirred. Four years, near to the day, since she left. The date of her leaving was the following week – 17 April – a dour anniversary he marked each year by getting roundly drunk. The previous year, he'd woken up on the floor beside the couch, having rolled off it at some point during the night, after blacking out. It was an almost scalding sensation, seeing her, being near her, after so long. But he also felt a tiny flicker of something akin to hope. Why was she here, out of the blue, like this? Could enough time have passed that she actually forgave him? Wanted to try again? No, he told himself. Not a chance. But still, the feeling was loose now, having bolted.

'Tea?' he asked.

'Sure, yeah.'

She sat at the table, the breadboard before her, a serrated knife, scattering of crumbs. As he filled the kettle, he saw her out of the corner of his eye corral the crumbs with her palm, sweep them off the table down by Sammy, for him to hoover up. His tail wagged anew. Once finished, he curled up under her chair.

Micheál was unsure whether to stay standing by the counter or sit at the table. In the end, he sat, not in the chair nearest her, nor furthest way, but in the middle ground. He wished again he'd had some warning. Even a shower would have him in a more confident standing.

A low grumble from the kettle.

'You look well, Nad; if you don't mind me saying.' She did: a glow and firmness to her that reminded him of her at her peak as a rower. Maybe she was back rowing with the club? He hoped so. When he imagined her, it was often beside or on the water; it had always seemed her natural element.

'You look tired,' she said. 'You're too young for all that grey, Mick.'

The rising grumble behind him. So many things he wanted to say. But how to come at them? How to even start?

'Did you watch the end of *Breaking Bad*?' He regrets the question as soon as it's asked.

'No, I couldn't, to be honest. Maybe someday.'

His gaze fell to the table, the few remaining crumbs. He ploughed on. 'Yeah, well, you should, when you get the chance. They actually stuck the landing pretty well.'

'Good to know.'

Behind him, a click and the grumbling stilled. He stood, moved towards the cupboard, relieved to find two clean cups. 'You still take your tea the same way?'

'No, actually, I've stopped having dairy. Do you have any alternatives?'

He shook his head. 'I'm not sure I even have any regular milk left, to be honest.'

'Black will be fine, then.'

When he turned around, cup in each hand, a spread of documents were set on the table. Where had they come from? Had she been holding them when she arrived? Still, to this day, he is unsure where they materialised from – not that it mattered. They existed now, even if they hadn't a moment before. He knew what they were, though he still asked. On some level, he needed her to say it.

'They are some documents you need to sign.'

'For what?'

'Our divorce.'

He felt a puncture in his chest, air slowly escaping. She saw it in him in that moment, the feeling that had been lost.

'Mick, you couldn't have thought –'

He waved her off. 'Of course not, no. Go on, explain them to me. I'll sign whatever you need.'

It turned out that you had to have lived apart for four of the previous five years before filing for divorce in Ireland, that was why she had waited until now before returning. Her father had told her to let their solicitor deal with it, but she'd wanted to come. She didn't say why. He guessed it had to do with closure. Putting a proper full stop on him, the headland, the life they could have had. He signed everything she put in front of him. Sammy, perhaps sensing something, had moved from under Nadine's chair to under his, his nose occasionally nudging the back of his legs.

'This'll get the ball rolling, anyway,' she said after he signed the final form.

'Good, good.'

Only then did she sip at her tea. Micheál sat back in his chair, looked again at the papers, at her. 'I'm still only half sure you're real, you know.'

Her expression grew hard to read. It reminded him of how she'd looked at him that first night they spoke, in the pub after the regatta. God, how nervous he'd been, walking her home. Looking back, he's not sure that feeling ever left him, all the time they were together.

'I'm real, alright.' She sat back and folded her arms. 'Why are you still here, Mick? On the headland, I mean. There are plenty of teaching jobs out there again. You could even go teach abroad, if you don't feel like working here. It's not good for you, you know, to stay on your own out here like this.'

'I'm not on my own.'

'The dog doesn't count.'

He felt the air in him, all but gone. It was causing a tightness in his chest, a deflation of skin against bone, organ. Soon he wouldn't be able to breathe.

'They need me,' he muttered.

'Who?' Then she understood. 'For fuck sake, Mick.'

'I'm all they have.'

For the first time, she seemed emotional. 'That's not true, Mick. It's not the 1960s anymore, where, you know, someone would "trip" and the shotgun would accidentally go off. It's not even like it was fifteen, twenty years ago, when you were growing up. People talk about this shit now, there are helplines, groups –'

'They need me.'

On her face in that moment was what he'd always expected to see, should they meet again: scorn, anger. 'Please. All those years when you were away in Limerick with me, all those years away from the headland, you didn't spare one thought for the people who came here. You're not helping these people, you're hiding in them; you're using them.'

He slid the final form across to her. A patch of tea grabbed at the right corner of the document. She moved it before the stain spread too far.

Gentler now, Nadine said, 'Mick, you stay here, living this life, you'll end up just like your parents.'

He stood. 'Thanks for the visit, Nad. It was good to see you again.'

She stood too. He was unprepared for her to cross the kitchen to him, raise a hand to his cheek. Her palm was a furnace. 'Take care of yourself, Mick, you hear me?'

'I do, yeah. I do. I mean, I will.'

78

One afternoon – he is unsure what day it is: Tuesday or Wednesday – he realises he hasn't enough energy for the day's walk. Instead, he plods to the door, leaves it open so Sammy can wander in and out as he chooses. Knows, as he does so, that he will do the same tomorrow, and each day after that.

LXXIX

The child would have had her eyes. He is sure of it.

80

Often, of late, Micheál finds his gaze lift above the TV – particularly, like now, during an ad break – and fall on Triskmore. This time, the mountain is a dark blue, bordering on purple, in the overcast evening light. It is not the mountain itself that he dwells on, though, but the Red Ditch that spines that mountain, and the others on the headland.

Many date it back to the Iron Age, while others place it in the Bronze Age. Either way, its beginnings are at least two and a half thousand years old, if not over three thousand. He imagines the starting point, or endpoint, of the earthwork up on Triskmore, nothing now but a shallow ditch with a low bank on one side. From his study of local history, he knows that there is more to this ditch. There is evidence of it stretching as far as Limerick, over a hundred miles away. No one is completely certain of the purpose of An Claí Rua. Some archaeologists think that the ditch was a boundary marker, used to divide clan territory, but most theorise that it was likely an ancient road. He often asks himself why the early inhabitants of this land would build a road to the end of this headland, stopping just short of precipitous cliffs.

Lately, he has wondered if An Claí Rua was built as a path for those unable to go on, a route to whatever afterlife they believed in then. Tír na nÓg, Hy-Brasil. What if, after thousands of years, this now-buried road is imprinted in the blood of those whose ancestors have lived and died in this land? Would that explain why people were drawn here? So many arrive without meaning to. They just walked without thinking, they say, as if guided by an invisible hand. God's hand, his mother used to say. Leading them to the brink, where they would find salvation. But Micheál sees in this land a path scoured into genes, an evolutionary pull. That could explain what brought them here. Why they keep coming.

In normal circumstances, anyway. Since Helena, no other visitor has come. Nearly two months now. Summer stirring. And nothing, no one. Still, the tension of a possible visit is ever-present. And, in recent days, he has noticed another feeling grow in him in response to the visitors' continued absence, one that he has avoided naming, as that would make it true.

Nadine's words return: *You're hiding in them; you're using them.*

Is he? She was right to say that he had given them little consideration while in Limerick. When he thought of the headland during those years, it was relief that he felt, to be away from the cliffs, his mother. What guilt he harboured during that time had nothing to do with the visitors but with Áine and Saoirse, leaving them behind. Even since his return to the headland, yes, his routine has revolved around the visitors, but his thoughts, when they do wander, tend to turn to Nadine, his childhood. What does that say about him? He never really dwells on the visitors, most of whom he can no longer name. Those he 'saved'. As if their problems, that dark weight or thread that brought them to the cliffs, were permanently gone when he drew them back from the edge. As if his refusal to stay in touch after they left his land was really to keep them from remembering the worst moment of their lives, and not to avoid him seeing that, in many instances, his help was not a cure but a cheap, poorly applied plaster, ready to fall off at the first bit of friction. That, in many cases, they may have tried again elsewhere. Some likely even succeeded.

And there were those he'd failed on the cliffs. Not just the homburg man, but the others who visited on his watch. The jumpers. Three in the nearly fifteen years. All young men. These names he remembers: Christopher Griffin, Myles Costello, Tomás O'Shea. Though why does he never really think about them? All along, he'd convinced himself that it was because it was too hard, that he needed to seal off thoughts of them to continue doing what he was doing. To help others. But now he wonders: is Nadine right? Does he actually care about these people? Or are they just a means for him to escape from the world, to punish himself for what he did to her, to his sisters? Even with Helena, did he care about what happened to her, or was he just sorry that he'd lost a distraction, someone who had kept that approaching leadenness at bay?

The ads end and another episode of *Community* takes his gaze from the mountain, An Claí Rua, visions of millennia of desperate visitors walking the trail to the sea. Finding at the end of it, now, only him.

LXXXI

Áine's expression the night he left, Saoirse's tears. Nadine's shock, on her knees among the wildflowers. The visitors without names, the visitors he failed. When he looks back on all that, he can only think: this is what I deserve.

This is as it should be.

82

It starts in his legs one night as Micheál lies on the couch. A restlessness. Unable to keep them still, he crosses and uncrosses them, kicks out as if doing the back stroke. And there's a fluttering in his chest. He feels as if all the energy that has been absent in him the past few weeks has surged into him all at once.

Heart pounding, he rises, an urgent need in him to burn it off. With little sound – Sammy is sleeping in his basket behind the TV – he puts on his runners, discarded by the door, and goes outside. The moon's shock is mirrored, distorted, by the sea. There is a giddiness in him that he can't explain. For the first time in years, he will run. His initial thought is for the road, feet pounding concrete, but his gaze soon turns towards wildflowers, the cliffs. A steep incline would more quickly empty him of this feeling. Maybe then he will be able to sleep.

He runs. On the first lap, he turns where wildflowers change to rock. On the second, lungs already burning, he ventures further on to rock. At the base of the incline, near the house, he can hear Sammy barking. Ignoring him, he begins another lap, a grasping burn in his chest now, legs jellying. He turns closer to the edge this time, the sound of crashing waves reaching him from below, swirling wind making a mess of his hair. On the next lap, just at the point of turning, he sees himself running a few steps further, till he feels the air, the wind – that suspended moment, awaiting the fall.

One more lap, he thinks, gasping for breath. One more lap and he will be done.

PART FIVE

83

Micheál is returning from the bathroom to his nest on the couch when he sees the figure walking up the hill towards the house. She is dressed in hiking boots, denim shorts and a sleeveless white T-shirt that highlights a deep tan and tattoo that sleeves her left arm. For a moment, he worries that she is a visitor, though her open, steady rise to the house makes this unlikely. Even after she has crested the hill, it takes him a shamefully long moment to recognise her.

A waft of hot air as he opens the front door, steps outside. The sea glitters behind her.

'Hi, Mick.'

'Jesus, Saoirse.' He takes a step towards her, then holds back. 'What are you doing here? How are you? What are you even doing here?'

'I've surprised you, anyway, I see.'

'You have.'

Something in her expression makes him think of his grubby tracksuit pants, stained T-shirt, the stink from his armpits. And then there is the state of the house. Still, he knows he has no choice but to invite her inside.

'Not today, anyway, if that's okay,' she says.

'You're sure?'

She nods. 'It was enough just to come out here from the village. Even walking up this hill towards the house, I thought I was going to turn back.'

'Right.'

'I'd take a glass of water off you, though.'

'No problem.'

Inside, he grabs a glass from the press and goes to the sink. He turns the cold water tap too much: water jets into the glass, spraying back up into his face, spattering his T-shirt. Sammy potters groggily into the kitchen. He'd been asleep in the visitors' room, a cool spot he likes when the days get too hot. The weather has been like this for nearly a month now: scalding, tropical, unrelenting. 'Go say hello to our guest there,' Micheál commands as he rushes past Sammy and down the hallway to the bathroom. The deodorant is next to the shaving cream; he can't remember which one he used more recently. It'd be too obvious if he changed the T-shirt, so he bombs himself with Old Spice instead.

When he returns outside, Saoirse is sitting on the windowsill, leaning over to rub an offered belly. 'This is the famous Sammy?' she asks, straightening to take the glass from Micheál.

'The one and only.'

'He's a beauty.'

'Doesn't he know it too.'

Saoirse takes a gulp of the water, squints out across the bay. A smattering of sailboats out there, white sails fluttering. 'You'd forget how stunning it is here. You'd struggle to find a more beautiful spot anywhere in the world, really, particularly when the weather's like this.'

'You'd know, I suppose; you've seen most of it at this point.'

'A fair bit, alright.'

Micheál considers sitting beside her on the sill, but decides to remain standing, back to the sun. He can feel the glare of it on his neck. The shock of her appearance is starting to wear off, questions gathering in its place.

'Why are you here, Saoirse? If this is about the selling up of the place –'

'It's got nothing to do with that, Mick.'

'Right.'

She hands him the glass, empty now. 'I'm staying in the village for the next while. I want you to come in tomorrow, have lunch with me in The Arms. Do you think you can do that?'

He shrugs, hoping it masks the rising tension in him. 'Ah, yeah, I suppose.'

'Say one o'clock?'

Another shrug. 'Okay.'

With that agreed, she stands. 'You can bring the beauty with you, too, if you want,' she says. A besotted Sammy follows her all the way down to the gate. By the time he returns, Micheál is sitting on the sill, wondering what just happened.

LXXXIV

Micheál had only seen Saoirse in person a handful of times since he moved to Limerick. The few times he visited home during those years, she was often at her friend Stephanie's house. At first, he'd felt hurt that she wasn't there to see him, but the more he thought about it, he was glad she seemed to be away from the house so much.

Then she moved to London and avoided returning home altogether. The only time he saw her during that period was one spring when he travelled to London with Nadine's father for a Six Nations game. They met outside the tube station at Leicester Square and she led him, already an expert in the inner city's mazey topography, to a too-cool-for-him café in Soho. He felt irredeemably parochial in his jeans and rugby jersey among all those stylish people.

When she sat down and took off her jacket, he immediately noticed the tattoo covering her arm. 'Jesus, that's something. You better not let Mam see that, anyway.'

'She won't, don't worry.'

An awkward lunch ensued. The rugby match wasn't to be played until the following day, so he had hoped that he and Saoirse would spend the afternoon wandering around the city, maybe visit a museum or two, see sights. But as soon as she'd finished her couscous and tofu salad, she said she had to go.

'I've work this evening.'

'Oh, right. I thought maybe you'd have the day off.'

'Afraid not; need to pay the rent.'

'Saoirse, if you need any help with money –'

'Don't, Mick.'

'Sorry.'

The last time he'd seen her in person was at Áine's wedding. They had tried Skype a couple of times since then, but soon gave up, blaming bad reception. In recent years, he has settled for Áine filling him in on the general outline of

Saoirse's life, resigned to the fact that he would not hear from her directly. Until now, anyway.

85

Micheál wakes to the sight of a white, stained neck of porcelain, the cold stick of linoleum against his right cheek, and a throbbing in his head. It takes a moment for the slanted view to shift into meaning. The toilet, the diamond-shaped pattern on the lino. He is on the floor of the bathroom.

His cheek peels away from the floor as he rises to a sitting position. He brings a hand to his forehead, near one of the corners where hair has started to retreat. That is the point at which the pain is sharpest. What had he even been doing? How had he ended up here? He remembers lying in bed, kept awake by a mixture of nerves and excitement over what tomorrow would bring. Saoirse's return was the last thing he'd expected, but here she is, wanting to see him. And while he knows that, on some level – despite her denial – this has to be about the house, he thinks that maybe he can live with that if it means getting to spend time with her.

But, yes, he'd been lying in bed, unable to sleep, when he felt the swell and press of his bladder and had stumbled to the bathroom. He remembers lifting the toilet seat – though for whose benefit, he doesn't know – and then a sudden light-headedness, a swaying, and his waking on the floor. He must have hit his head against the toilet on the way down. Lucky he didn't break his nose, knock out teeth, strike a temple.

He rises unsteadily to his feet. The sounds out of him could as easily come from a man twice his age. But this is something Micheál has found himself thinking about of late. Are you only old when you have lived a long life, or are you old when you feel you're near your limit, regardless of years? Was there a difference? Either way, you might only have a small spit of time left. And Micheál knows one thing to be true: lately, he feels ancient.

He shuffles to the mirror over the sink, sees the red mound already stretching the skin of his forehead, as if something is trying to erupt from his head. No doubt about it, he thinks, touching his forehead and wincing. This is going to leave a mark.

LXXXVI

Saoirse must have only been eight or nine when, one evening at dinner, she pushed aside the plate of chicken drumsticks, mashed carrots and boiled potatoes before her and declared that she would no longer eat meat. Micheál remembers scoffing along with Áine as Saoirse's face brightened in a mix of embarrassment and obstinacy. In the days and weeks that followed, both he and Áine became allies, for once, in a bid to torment Saoirse: exaggerating their chewing of chicken or cod or pork opposite her at the kitchen table, leaving a packet of rashers under her pillow one night, and once stuffing slices of Ballyfree ham into the sandwich for her packed lunch.

Only their mother supported her, said it was important to respect her beliefs. Though even her support had limits. One weekend, Saoirse spent the whole afternoon in her room, Micheál remembers, despite the fine weather. She had music on loud enough that he'd thought she was imitating Áine. His mother went to her room in the late afternoon, likely to tell her to turn it down, when Micheál heard a scream. He ran down to Saoirse's bedroom, found his mother with a hand to her forehead. 'What are the Spillanes going to say to this?' He saw the defiance on Saoirse's face as he followed his mother's gaze. Nested in the bottom of the wardrobe, munching contentedly on iceberg lettuce, was one of the Spillanes' lambs. 'It wanted to be free,' Saoirse said.

87

Micheál slaps Factor 50 on every exposed part of himself before he struggles on to the bike and starts towards the village. His legs ache at once.

Bales of hay, long since stacked, stand in the surrounding fields like ancient markers. Ahead, the road shimmers. Near the village, he begins to notice the changes that the season brings to the summer homes along the road: cars parked in driveways, trampolines in front gardens, bikes sprawled against wall, patio door, pavement. Burst water balloons are scattered on the road between two homes, the water long since dried up. As expected, the village is bloated with holidayers and day trippers. On either side, a flurry of pale or red skin, sunglasses, the scent of sunscreen. With the cycle, Micheál hopes that his lotion hasn't been sweated off him.

As he locks the bike against a parking sign by the castle gateway, he feels a little dizzy. This has happened more regularly of late. It must be the heat. Or else he needs to get back into the habit of cycling. Walking across the square towards The Arms, he takes in the view of the coast. The tide is about halfway out, the exposed strand covered with people seemingly as far as the Black Rock. The car park behind the strand is full, the overflow snaking up both sides of the road. Cars are parked all along Main Street, too. Micheál feels his breathing quicken again, and knows this time that he cannot blame the cycling or the heat.

Saoirse has somehow managed to procure a two-person table outside the pub. She rises when she sees him and gives him a brief hug. 'What happened there?' she asks, nodding towards his forehead.

Micheál stops himself from bringing his hand to the mark; he knows well that it's still tender to the touch. 'Smacked it off the press by the sink this morning. Was still half asleep.'

'Not the best start to your day.'

He laughs. 'No, it definitely was not.'

Already he can tell that there is less tension in her today; sensing this, some of the unease lifts in him. A waitress comes out, forehead a blush of spots, and he orders a cider. Saoirse has a green tea and glass of water. A book rests on the table between them, cover-down. He sees the words 'climate' and 'environment' several times on the blurb.

'Any good?' he asks.

'Infuriating.'

'In a good or bad way?'

'Is there a good way to be infuriated?'

'Fair point.'

His pint arrives and he drinks deep. Nothing beats a cider in this weather. A few more sips might even take the edge off being around this many people. A red-faced man in a Dublin jersey at a nearby table has a hyena laugh that has already started to grate. All around, there seem to be children crying.

'Where are you staying, by the way?'

She hesitates. 'With Brenda.'

'Oh, right.'

'Áine set it up for me. She has me in the attic room; you could fit a bloody orchestra in that space, it's huge. Don't know why she doesn't rent it out, she'd make herself a tidy sum, I'd say.'

He takes another sip of the drink as he feels his cheeks flush.

'No, that sounds good, alright. Good of Brenda to put you up. Surprised there's enough room, with Aengus in there too these days.'

'Well, that isn't an issue anymore; they broke up a couple of months back.'

He frowns into his pint. A wasp buzzes over his head, drawn near by the scent of the cider.

'I'm starting a job in Tralee tomorrow. I'm doing a few hours a week in the English college in the IT. They need a hand with some of the summer students.'

'You're around for a while, so?' he asks, surprised.

'Well, the job is there for the summer, if I want it, but we'll see. I'll give it a few weeks, anyway.'

The wasp lands on the table, not far from his pint. He places a beer mat over the top of the glass as he returns his attention to his sister. The urge to ask why she is here rises in him again. It has to, at least in part, be about the house.

'How's that guy you were seeing a while back? The guy with the very American name.'

'Jared?'

'That's the one.'

She laughs. 'God, yeah, he's long gone. Back in America now. To be fair to him, he wasn't as annoying as his name suggests.'

'I'm sure,' he says, lifting the beer mat off the pint glass, the wasp now gone. Across the bay, a gorse fire has started to burn on the shoulder of the Slieve Mish Mountains. Farmers say it's essential, that it clears away dead scrub for fresh growth, but all he can think of are the wild-eyed animals caught in the smoke, the wind-fanned flames. Unsure what way to turn; unsure if there even is a way out anymore.

LXXXVIII

Brenda came to the house often during the school years. She and Áine had been best friends all the way through primary school, and their friendship only strengthened as they transitioned into secondary, taking the same bus as Micheál into Tralee, where they both attended the Presentation Secondary School.

They claimed to be studying on the evenings she visited, though most of their time seemed to be spent laughing in Áine's room, making jam sandwiches in the kitchen, or hitting tennis balls off the side of the house with their mother's old wooden racket, when the weather allowed.

One evening, as Micheál did his homework in his bedroom, he felt eyes on him. He turned around and saw Brenda peeking in from the hallway through the half-opened door. She still had her school uniform on, the check-pattern, ankle-length skirt and navy, round-necked jumper; a slice of white bread spattered red held delicately in her hand.

'What?' Micheál asked.

She hesitated a moment, then said, 'You can sit with us, if you want.'

It took him a moment to understand what she was talking about. The bus. Tuan and Stephen were no longer friends with him. This meant sitting by himself at the front of the bus.

Micheál stood and closed the door. It was a while before he heard her walk away.

Later, Áine told him that Brenda had served Stephen one Saturday in the newsagents during that time. He was buying a loose bag of penny sweets: Refreshers, Apple Jacks, Fizzy Colas. According to Áine, when Stephen was distracted, Brenda knelt down out of sight behind the counter and spat into his bag. Then she took his money and handed him his sweets.

89

Micheál gathers the cleaning supplies bought before Áine's visit last autumn on the kitchen table. Most still have enough in them for another big clean. No need to cycle into the heaving village. Now, he just has to set his mind for the job ahead. He's never let things get this bad before.

Saoirse has her first day teaching in the English-language school today, but promised that she will travel out to the house tomorrow. 'I might even come inside this time,' she said, a forced smile on her face. 'It's kind of like exposure therapy, isn't it? A little more each time.' He was unsure if the exposure referred to the house, the cliffs, or him. Likely, all of them.

Before he starts cleaning, he opens the windows throughout the house, wedges the front door open with a chair. His nose has grown too used to the place to pick up any smell, but there must be something strong lodged in the place, months now without an open window, the dirty plates and gone-off food – not to mention his and Sammy's grubby states. If he gets a chance, he'll give the dog a bath. It is long overdue. As if he can sense this possibility, Sammy is nowhere in sight.

He begins with the ware. It's frustrating how quickly it piles up, even when living by yourself. Next, he starts on the hoovering, and this brings Sammy out from his hiding spot in Micheál's bedroom. He barks down the length of the hallway, defiant, though not eager to come any closer. Sammy and the hoover have always had a fractious relationship.

So Brenda is single again. He has tried not to think about this, but his mind returns to it as he cleans. A couple of months ago, Saoirse said. So not too long after her birthday. He wonders who did the breaking up. If Aengus had taken off again, got a job in Cork, Dublin; or maybe Brenda had finally realised they were a poor match.

He sprays the counters, begins to scrub at the surface. Like before, some of the stains refuse to give way; if anything, the scrubbing seems to print them more firmly into the counter. He scrubs harder; he wants the place to be perfect. Part of him struggles to believe that Saoirse has returned, that she will actually be here, spending time with him, tomorrow. That she may even be here for the entire summer. Maybe longer, who knows? He wonders if he should prepare her bedroom, in case she decides to stay the night.

A sudden burst of movement out the sink window. He stops scrubbing. A small bird has landed on the sill. Micheál remains motionless so as not to disturb it, force it back into flight. It ducks its beak briefly in under its wing, tilts its head upwards, calls out. The grey-green back, the slight tinge of yellow on its throat and chest, its slender pink legs. It's a warbler, he is sure, though the subspecies is hard to call. It's either a chiffchaff or a willow warbler; they are very similar in size and appearance. Though that yellow stripe – that's a feature of the willow warbler, isn't it? And the chiffchaff's legs tend to be darker. Yes, it must be a willow warbler.

XC

He remembers sitting outside, reading, on the grass by the line, on a summer's afternoon. He must have been thirteen, maybe fourteen. His mother sat on the windowsill, taking in the sun, while Saoirse wandered among the wildflowers, making chains, a crown. A bird, close though not visible, lets out a musical call, a rising note.

'Do you hear that?' his mother asked.

'What?'

'The birdsong. Can you name the bird? It's a regular around here.'

He shrugged.

His mother stood and went into the house. Moments later, she returned and sat next to him with a thick book: *Complete Irish Wildlife.* 'Your father used to always say, and I agree with him, that you should know as much as you can about the place in which you live – its history, its geography, the animals and plants. It's how you become rooted; it'll help you feel more strongly like you belong here.'

For a while, he tried. He kept the book near at hand, learned that the birds he often saw plummet to the sea were gannets, how there were different types of seagull, crow. That the sleek-looking animals he sometimes saw in the water, and was unsure if they were bird or some sort of sea creature, were called cormorants. He soon lost interest, though, particularly as his resentment grew. Why learn more about a landscape he wanted to escape? When he returned, he tried again, and was surprised to find a growing satisfaction in naming the birds he saw, noting them down. Though, for all that enjoyment, when he looks at the names and the dates in his notebooks, he doubts now that the promised feeling of belonging will ever come.

The front door is still wedged open, airing the place out, when Saoirse arrives in the evening. Supper time, as their mother would have called it, the Angelus echoing from the TV. Micheál is busy dumping the pile of dirty clothes from his bedroom floor into the wardrobe when he hears her call out. Reaching the kitchen, he finds her still at the entrance, Sammy in a near-frenzy by her side. 'Come in, come in,' he says, and winces, knowing that he sounded like his mother in that moment; she had always said that in the same sing-song fashion whenever a regular visitor dawdled at the open door.

'What sort of tea would you like? I've a decent selection there if you want to take a look,' he says, pointing towards an array of packages by the kettle.

While cleaning yesterday, it struck him that he had no real options for her to eat or drink during her visit, given that she was a vegan. He waited until after seven o'clock, when the village would be quieter, the heat less intense, and Brenda's closed, before cycling in to Costcutter. Oreos are dairy-free, it turns out. And Bourbon Creams. He couldn't believe how many of the crisps had dairy in them. Why was there a need to put dairy in Taytos? He'd bought a pack of the green tea he'd seen her drinking, and some camomile and pepper-mint, too.

'I'll just have Barry's,' she says, stepping inside.

'Will I add sugar, some milk? I have coconut milk, if you'd like that?'

Standing by the table, a hand grasping the back of one

of the chairs, she surveys the room. 'Black is fine,' she says distractedly. 'No sugar.'

Without a word, she walks out of the kitchen and into the hallway, Sammy trailing behind. Micheál lets her be and begins setting the table. He had bought some sourdough bread, too, and sunflower spread; hopefully all this would satisfy her.

He hears Saoirse make her way into different rooms. She spends the longest time in her old bedroom. When she returns to the kitchen, he sees that the earlier uncertainty is gone from her expression. She looks at the offering on the table and smiles. 'Oreos are my favourite; how did you know?'

'Lucky guess.'

Her gaze is drawn to it throughout the meal, he notices, but she waits until after they have eaten to ask the question.

'Is that mam's jumper?'

The green woollen top is still cast over the chair nearest the hallway, left there by Helena the morning she departed. He has been unable to touch it since.

'Yeah, do you want it?'

'I don't want anything that belonged to that woman.'

She takes a packet of cigarettes, Camel Blues, from her purse, and with a gesture asks if it's okay for her to light up. He nods and the cigarette flares. He withholds what he wants to say until the cigarette is finished, and some of the food eaten.

'She wasn't all bad, you know.'

'Wasn't she?' Saoirse sits back in the chair, looks around the room. 'I don't know how you can stand living here again. I keep expecting her to jump out from behind a curtain with some Mad Valley water or appear in the TV like a poltergeist.'

Micheál nods. He sometimes wishes their story was as obvious and easy as a haunting: blood on the walls, objects flying, shattering.

'It's not so bad, after you give it some time. All that stuff is in the past, anyway.'

Saoirse scoffs. 'So the past and the present are two different states, is that what you're telling me? With you here, back in this house, with the visitors – and you're telling me that the past is dealt with? Even at the best of times, keeping the past at bay is like – what's that game? You see it all the time in American TV shows, every time they go to a fun fair. Whack-a-mole! It's like whack-a-mole. And being stuck back here, you have no hope of keeping them all in their holes.'

'I manage.'

'Doesn't look like it,' she says. 'You don't look well, Mick.'

'Well, at least if I drop dead, you'd get the house, I suppose.' He meant that to sound like a joke, but knows that he failed.

Smoke veils her face, disperses. 'Halloran raised his offer, by the way. He really wants this place, according to Áine.'

A gust of anger blows up out of him. 'You are just here for the house, aren't you? You all think I can be turned.'

Her exhalation has the hint of a sigh. 'There can be more than one reason for my being here, Mick. I can be here for the house. I can be here for myself, I can even be here for you, you eejit.' She stubs the cigarette out on the empty plate and stands. 'I better head back before it gets dark.'

He follows her to the door, notes a surprising nip to the air. 'Are you sure you don't want mam's jumper, even just for the walk in?'

He isn't quite sure why he offers it again. He knows the answer before she even says it.

She shakes her head, states simply: 'You give me that jumper, I'll burn it – or throw it off those fucking cliffs.'

She begins to walk down towards the gate.

'You'll come back in a few days?' He blushes, knows how desperate he sounds.

She turns to him, sighs. 'I will, Mick. I'll be out again soon. I promise.'

XCII

Not long after the move out to the headland, his mother arrived back from Tralee with a bag full of wildflower seeds. Each type of seed in its own packet, the name written across it in English and some also in Latin: Corncockle/*Agrostemma githago*, Ox-eye Daisy/*Leucanthemum vulgare*, Larkspur 'Galilee Pink', Cowslip, *Gypsophilia elegans*, Ragged Robin. She gathered the family together, except his grandmother, who was confined mostly to her bed at that point.

'Okay, this is a family activity. We're all going to go into the field and spread these up as far as the cliffs. We want to cover as much ground as we can. Is everyone with me?'

His father motioned for Micheál and Áine to nod.

'Yes,' they both said. Micheál took six seed packets from the table; Áine, after watching him, took seven.

Outside, they wandered the field, scattering seeds. His mother held Saoirse in her arms, who stuck a pudgy hand into a packet, dropped seeds to the ground. Once she put some in her mouth, and his mother made her spit them out into her open palm. She then knelt down and rubbed spit and seed into earth. Near the cliffs, he heard his mother say something to his father that he didn't understand at the time: 'It's important they see that there's beauty in the world, even at its darkest points. You never know, a bit more beauty under their noses might still their feet. Even a moment's hesitation could be all the difference.'

93

Micheál takes his phone from his pocket, scrolls through the numbers. Saoirse had left a few hours earlier, but he has been unable to get what she said about their mother out of his mind. He suspects this is a bad idea, is certain of it, in fact, but still he thumbs the name, hears it dial.

'Have you changed your mind?' Áine asks.

Down the line, he can hear the sound of sirens, barked orders, shooting.

'No.'

'I don't want to hear from you then, Mick; not until you've decided to give up that place.'

'Was she good, do you think?'

'Who?'

'Mam.'

'Jesus, Mick.'

'Was she, though?'

'I don't know. I mean, she may have been a good person, in some ways. She was just a terrible mother.'

'She did love us, though.'

He was certain of that much. She said it often during his childhood, said it on their rare meetings after he'd departed the headland; she said it on the phone at the end of every conversation. Sure, there were times when it had sounded like a threat, or a damning verdict, but it was clear that she meant it.

More gunfire, followed by what sounded like an explosion.

'Yes, Mick, but she loved them more. Or, I don't know, she loved what helping them gave her. She wanted to feel like she was making a difference, that she had meaning, I think. And you've only gone and fallen for the same trap, haven't you, you bollox. Probably makes you feel a little less like you've fucked up your life.'

'Áine.'

'Don't call again until you've agreed to sell. I mean, for fuck's sake, Mick, this isn't just for me and mine, d'you know? This could really change everything for you, too, if you let it.'

She hangs up before he has a chance to respond.

XCIV

He last spoke to his mother about a fortnight before her death. The conversation followed a familiar pattern: How was Nadine? How was work? Any news from the headland?

He had thought they would at some point have an open conversation about everything, but her sudden death denied him that. In the years since, he has imagined different versions of a final confrontation. Often, it happened at the hospital, Micheál making it there just in time. Other times, he had decided for unclear reasons to drive down to the headland the preceding night, finding her shortly after her collapse, cold but conscious on the kitchen floor. After calling an ambulance, he would carry her to the couch, lie her down. There she was, helpless, ready for interrogation.

Sometimes he was angry with her. He shouted, roared, kicked over the coffee table. Other times, he pleaded, or remained almost aloof in his questioning, detached. Why did you drag me into this? Why didn't you give me a choice? Why didn't you take us away from here, protect us, give us a normal life? Even in these, his fantasies, she always held out. He couldn't even get this imagined version of her to voice his guesses. That it was God's work. That she knew he was strong enough, her Superman. She knew it would do him good to do good. There always needs to be two; she couldn't do it alone. Whatever way he asked, wherever he imagined the confrontation, she remained silent, her expression unreadable.

95

The sun rises so early these mornings. Throughout the night, even, a blue-purple hue clings to the fringes of the western sky, as if the sun never quite departs. Micheál waits an hour after sunrise – which has sometimes brought a visitor, after a long dark night – before getting, with difficulty, on to his bike. He had checked the tide charts the night before; it should be at its lowest point when he reaches the strand.

As he cycles, he looks in at farmland, garden. The grass has stopped growing now, has turned a burnt brown in patches. A nationwide hosepipe ban has been put in place, he saw online last night. Drought conditions have been declared in several counties, including Kerry. The reservoir down by Killorglin is reported to be at a near-record low. And Met Éireann are not yet forecasting an end to the heatwave. At times, he swears he can almost hear the parched earth, crying out for a reprieve. An end to its suffering.

The village is blessedly empty. He stops pedalling as he reaches the winding road down to the car park, momentum from the decline taking him on to the stone walkway and down to the strand. The upper reaches of the strand are pebble-heavy and the sand is soft, but soon he finds firmer terrain and pedals towards his destination, the morning air cool and heavy with the scent of seaweed. The tide is so far out that you'd half-worry a tsunami is on the way.

The wreck, near the retreated shoreline, is still partly sunk in sand. Jagged shafts of wood, darkened by centuries under water, jut out like the ribcage of some giant, prehistoric creature. Part of the bow has resurfaced, too – a fractured horn. Once off his bike, he crouches beside the ship. It smells of iodine and rot. Fresh-looking marks and cuts decorate parts of the ship. He's read online how some people have come out here, hacked and torn pieces of wood, fled with souvenirs.

Circling the wreck, he has a sudden urge to rebury it, but recognises that would be pointless. Regardless of what is done now, he knows, it will keep resurfacing.

XCVI

The past is always there, anyway, even when you can't see it. What's more, it seems grooved into this patch of land and sea. By some counts, over two hundred ships have been wrecked in the bay – and those are just the recorded losses, starting with the British-flagged *York* in October 1758, run aground among the Seven Hogs. Ships keep wrecking, visitors keep visiting – all the mistakes repeat.

97

He knows what day it is. If anything, he surprises himself by making it as far as midday before breaking. He checks June's profile first. Already, she has posted several photos. In the first, Nadine is in a dressing gown, hair encased in curlers, her mouth captured mid-expletive, front teeth biting down on bottom lip, eyes smiling, as she's surprised by the camera. There's another photo of a tray of mimosas. June has also photographed Nadine's mother, wearing an identical dressing gown to Nadine. She looks well, little different from when he last saw her, except that she has let her hair grey. He checks the husband-to-be's profile. He has posted no photos, though he was tagged in a photo yesterday: himself and two friends at a paintball arena, dressed in full camouflage and aiming a gun at the camera. The photo comes with the caption: 'Preparation for married life.'

He can't help it; he returns to social media throughout the day. June stops posting once the ceremony begins, but the groom is tagged in a number of photos, and other attendees have public profiles. The ceremony is small – 'intimate' is probably the word they'd use – and held in a hotel in Dún Laoghaire. It makes sense, he thinks, since she's already done the traditional church wedding. Nadine's father's complexion is startlingly red. He better still be taking those blood-pressure tablets. Nadine looks beautiful in a cream silk dress. He wonders if her tan is real or fake. During college, she used to ask him to spread fake tan across her back, the parts she was unable to reach. The stink and stain of the stuff on his hands afterwards – it'd linger for hours, and, though he disliked the smell, he'd find himself bringing his hand to his nose, breathing deep. A photo of Nadine and the groom during the ceremony shows a ribbon being tied around their clasped hands. Her godmother, Sandra, posts a video of the vows. *I am happy for her*, he reminds himself. *I am happy for her*. After he says it a few more times, a realisation: it is, at least partly, the truth.

A knock on the door, mid-afternoon, not long after the ceremony ends. He'd been too absorbed to notice anyone climb towards the house. He snaps the lid of his laptop shut, hauls himself with considerable effort off the couch.

Saoirse grins, lifts a plastic bag into the air, as if doing a bicep curl. It is one of the blue bags he recognises from Brenda's shop. Inside it is an eight-pack of cider.

'We didn't agree to meet up today, did we?' he asks.

Sammy bursts past him, jumps on Saoirse. She laughs, nearly knocked over by the force of him. 'Ah, well, no, but it turned out that I'd the day off and I figured it's a day for sitting outside with a few cans, isn't it?' She sweeps a hand across the sparkling bay, blue sky.

She knows what day it is, Micheál realises. She's travelled out to distract him.

'Come in, come in,' he says, an unfamiliar feeling in his chest. 'I'll never say no to cider on a fine day.'

XCVIII

How excited he'd been, that morning. There had been no nerves on his part, only the nagging concern that she might change her mind. The relief he'd felt when he saw her at the entrance of the church, her dress such a shade of white it seemed to almost glow.

Afterwards, outside the church, he remembers standing for photos with his mother and Áine. Saoirse had been unable to make it: exam preparation, she'd said. Both looked beautiful, he told them. 'You're looking sharp yourself,' Áine said. 'I don't know how you lucked out finding a woman like Nadine, so make sure not to do something stupid and feck it up.' He nodded. 'I won't.'

At the hotel, he watched his mother speak with Nadine's

parents, an awkwardness in him that he couldn't explain. They seemed to get on, which was what mattered, he reminded himself. Áine introduced him to Brian, her boyfriend of six months. 'Funny time for a first meeting,' Micheál said. 'Our paths don't cross as much as they should,' Áine said. He chose to ignore the barb in that.

His mother lasted until just after the first dance before she approached him, said she was leaving.

'I thought you were staying the night? We've a room set out for you. And how are you going to get home anyway?'

'Áine's boyfriend is going to drive us. He doesn't drink, what with his soccer. And it's a long way down, Micheál. You know that. We can't leave it too late.'

After their departure, he did try to disguise how hurt he felt, but he must have done a terrible job, as people kept asking him if he was okay. A drunk cousin, Jamesie, threw his arm around his shoulder, said: 'Jesus, lad, are you regretting it already? They'll throw you in the *Guinness Book of World Records* if you divorce her this fast.' It was his own fault, he knew; thinking that, for one night, she'd choose him over the visitors.

His mother didn't live long enough to see Áine married. He was back on the headland by then, his own marriage over. The ceremony was in Macroom, her husband's parish, as Áine did not want to have it in Ballyheigue. Brian had filled out since they'd first met, a beard adding some much-needed years. Saoirse made this wedding, at least. They spoke a bit, but kept things general, safe – though she did say that she was sorry to hear about Nadine. 'It's my own fault,' he said. 'Sounds like it, alright,' she replied.

It was during the speeches that he found himself checking the time on his phone. Realising what he was doing, he stuffed his phone in his pocket, resisted the urge to take it out again. He forced himself to stay until well into the night, though the pull in him was like a spring tide by the time the band finished and DJ started.

On the dance floor, Saoirse was twirling about with Brenda, and Áine was talking to Brian's parents. He decided not to disturb them, felt it better to slip away. Áine never mentioned his leaving the wedding, but he now wonders if she thought, as he had done when his mother left: *Not even for one night?*

99

When the film finishes, both Micheál and Saoirse sit on the couch in silence, the pinks and golds of the evening light painting the headland outside. She'd been appalled to hear that he'd never seen *Princess Mononoke*. The only Studio Ghibli film he'd watched was *Spirited Away*. 'Everyone's seen that one!' she said, taking his laptop from the coffee table. He snatched it from her, shut down the window full of wedding pictures, and found a good-quality stream with subtitles.

'Well, what do you think?' Saoirse asks. She says it in such a way that he knows if he responds negatively, she'll never speak to him again. No fear of that, though; he had loved it.

'Powerful stuff, alright. Violent, though. Can't imagine being allowed to watch that when we were growing up.'

She laughs. 'Not a chance, no. I mean, there definitely weren't anywhere near as many beheadings in *Animaniacs*.'

Before starting the film, Saoirse had talked about visiting the Studio Ghibli museum in Tokyo. This would have been during her two years teaching in Japan. She'd gone with Jared, and they'd wandered about, taking photos of each other next to life-size models of characters from their films. Later that evening, after dinner, they started to walk back towards the hotel. They were strolling through a park when the ground began to tremble, then shake violently. There was a poplar nearby, and the leaves started to fall, and as she looked up at them she could see that the skyscrapers beyond the park were swaying. The whole world shook. 'And it was this moment that made me realise that we live on something alive, like actually alive; and it can get angry.'

As she watches the slow drain of evening light outside, she asks, 'Speaking of so-called kids' shows, do you remember *Dinosaurs*?'

'Was that the one about the family of dinosaurs? But they had jobs and lived in normal houses and all that?'

'Yeah, that's it. Do you remember the ending?'

Micheál scratches his chin. 'God, vaguely. Something bleak? What happened, again?'

'They all fucking die! And it's not even by asteroid. The dad in the show takes over this big multinational company – which he's wanted to do for the entire run of the show – but by accident he leads the company into bringing about a new ice age! In the early nineties you've a kids' show that predicted the end of civilisation through mismanagement and big business. Who would have thought *Dinosaurs* would be the most prescient creative work of the last fifty years!'

Her voice is animated by the same enthusiasm he remembers her bringing to her art. Does she ever draw anymore, he wonders, but is too afraid to ask. Micheál looks out the window, magic hour starting to wane. 'You should probably be heading off if you want to get back to Brenda's before it gets dark. You don't want to be walking the roads at night; not when there are so many tourists around.'

Saoirse looks down at the empty cup she's holding in her hands. 'I was thinking, if it's alright, that I might stay here tonight. '

'Are you sure?'

'Yeah, I think so.'

Micheál lifts himself off the couch, careful to avoid a sleeping Sammy by his feet. 'I'll go set up your room, so.'

A wry smile. 'Thanks, though it's not really my room, is it?'

'What do you mean?'

'Well, everyone just called it "the visitors' room", didn't they, when we were growing up. Even Mam and Dad. It was like I was just keeping it warm for them.'

Micheál hesitates, unsure what to say. Then he makes for the hallway. 'There are some fresh sheets in the hot press; I'll get them for you.'

As he walks through the kitchen, Saoirse asks, 'So, you really liked the movie, Mick?'

He nods. 'I loved it, yeah.'

Later that night, Micheál lies in his bed, staring at the ceiling. The same ceiling his grandparents stared up at, his parents too. He needs sleep but knows by now that it won't come.

He would like to sneak to the sitting room, turn on the TV – there are usually some *30 Rock* reruns on E4 around this time – but the last thing he wants is to disturb Saoirse. Though she has seemed more comfortable with each visit, he knows that she still struggles with coming here. Before bed, she had spotted one of his notebooks on the kitchen counter, picked it up and leafed through the pages.

'So you do think about getting away from here.'

'Why do you say that?'

She placed the notebook back down on the counter. 'Well, you have a journal full of all these birds and ships. Things that appear here, sure, but things that also all get to leave. Doesn't seem like a coincidence.'

Near dawn, he hears movement from the hallway, the kitchen – quiet, careful steps that most would miss. The front door opens, stays open. Is she leaving? Why would she leave without saying goodbye? And why leave the front door open? A shadow passes his window, moving in the direction of the cliffs. There is no real view of the rise to the cliffs from his window, so he climbs out of his bed and, chest tightening, runs into Áine's old room.

It takes him a few moments to make her out in the half-light. She stands in a knee-length T-shirt among the wildflowers, eyes cast out across the bay, a deformed half-moon snared in the water just beyond Illauntannig. Then, in one swift movement, she hikes her T-shirt up over her waist, squats and pisses on grass, wildflower, morning dew.

Micheál looks away, though waits until she starts back

towards the house before returning to his bedroom. He is under the blankets by the time he hears the front door close, the patter of bare feet along the hallway. Why had she done that? Why had she not used the toilet? He thinks back to the previous evening. Had she used the bathroom then? She must have, given the cider. But he just remembers her going outside for cigarette breaks during the movie. Looking back, had she used the bathroom in any of her visits this summer? He can't remember. He turns on to his side, wills himself to get at least some sleep. But all that's in his head now is his sister, squatting among the wildflowers.

C

He visited New York with Nadine not long before the recession hit. They rented an apartment in Brooklyn for the period, a one-bed 'hipster pad', as he called it. Neither of them could deal with the humidity the first night, clothes and sheets discarded, fan on full blast. The one time he tried to roll towards her, she guffawed: 'Don't you fucking dare; you're like a radiator in normal weather, never mind now.'

They did all the typical first-time-in-New-York things: went to the top of the Empire State Building, the Statue of Liberty, boat ride in Central Park, visited the MET, MOMA; they even went to a baseball game at Yankee Stadium, though both found the game itself tedious. They left at the bottom of the sixth. It was maybe on the third or fourth day, as they rode the subway, that Nadine made the comment. How much brighter he seemed since arriving. No more Mopey Micheál.

'Work must have been stressing you out the last while?' she asked.

He shrugged. 'I suppose.'

Afterwards, he mulled it over. He was feeling lighter, happier, but did that have to do with getting away from work? Everything was fine on that front. The workload was manageable; the children were relatively well behaved, though that Leahy child was a nuisance. No, his distance from work wasn't the issue.

It was only on the last day or so of the holiday, as he felt the muscles in his shoulders begin to tense, and his mind drift repeatedly towards home, that he realised the cause. Kerry Head. He thought Limerick was far enough away, but clearly it was still a presence in his head. The idea that, at any moment, she might find a way to drag him back to the headland. Only in New York – the furthest he'd ever been from home – did he notice the absence of it. It made him think of Saoirse, who had left London the previous year with a TEFL certificate to go teach in Corsica, and was about to take a teaching role in Dubai. He wondered if this was how she felt, if that was why she kept moving further from the reach of home.

101

Micheál sits on the remnants of the fort and looks out to sea. It is another scorcher of a day, the sea calm, spotted with pleasure craft. A speedboat races towards the Maharees, a white trail behind it, at first clear, then fading to nothing. Sammy barks in the overgrowth nearby, catching a scent.

Micheál runs a hand over the fort wall, the stone cool despite the glare of the sun. The earth around the fort has pared back in the deep heat of the past month, giving a stronger hint at what lies beneath the surface. It's been like this all over the country. He's seen pictures online: aerial shots of the outlines of ringforts suddenly reappearing in fields, granges, lost settlements. The land's own time falling in on itself, the past returning.

As he rests on the wall, he takes the letter from his jeans pocket. It had arrived that morning, and for once was not from Áine's solicitor. He reads it again:

Dear M.,

Hope you're well and continue to sleep like you did on the night I left. Such snores – you nearly took the roof from the house! I am staying with my sister, Cathy (address above). Have started treatment. A pain, but am holding up so far. Sister has been a blessing. Thank you for everything, Micheál. Allow yourself more nights of blissful, roof-threatening sleep like you had the night of the heron.

Will write again soon. Please do the same, if you've the time.

H

He pockets the letter, makes for the house. Walking along the road, he has to step in towards the ditch several times to allow cars to pass, some with car regs from counties other than Kerry, two with the blue and yellow stars of the EU, and one with the yellow reg of the UK. The 'Wild Atlantic Way' route brings a lot more traffic to the headland at this time of year.

Near the house, Micheál sees a sheep far ahead on the road. As he nears, it is clear that there is something odd in its movement, its shape. He squints as Sammy tucks in behind him, unsure what to make of the creature ahead. It's not a sheep, he realises, but a llama. The animal stops perhaps two hundred metres away, startled by Micheál and Sammy. Something in this image, as he takes it in, seems to sum up everything about the world as it is now: off-kilter, panicked, absurd. And he can't help it; he starts laughing, even as the llama turns and runs away.

CII

He keeps returning to that image of his mother, no more than six or seven, standing amid the desecrated remains of a snowman in their neighbour's back yard. He has imagined her multiple ways when found red-handed by the Sullivans – smiling, growling, contrite, defiant – but he is beginning to understand: he'll never know what expression she wore. He'll never know which version of her is true.

103

The visitor arrives at the point where late afternoon meets early evening. It is late in the day, but at this time of year sunset is still hours away. Micheál is in the process of serving Saoirse dinner – breaded tofu with asparagus and baby potatoes – when he sees the man out the inland-facing window. It is clear from the way he staggers up the hill that he is drunk.

Shit, he thinks, looking at Saoirse, who sits at the kitchen table, staring at her iPhone. He picks up his jumper from the back of the chair, the flashlight from the counter. Always be prepared for a long visit, his mother said.

Saoirse looks up at him, sees the jumper and flashlight. The change in her expression brings a swell of pain to his chest.

'I'm sorry,' he says, opening the front door.

CIV

It was raining the morning his mother drove him to the bus station in Tralee, his rucksack splayed across the back seat, stuffed with clothes and books. The trip was silent but for the squeaking wipers as far as Ardfert, when he broke: 'I'll be home most weekends.' He had thought that would appease her, but, if anything, her demeanour grew colder; she seemed to almost be curling in on herself as she glared out the fogged-up windscreen. At the station, he hesitated before getting out of the car, though the bus looked ready to depart. He is still unsure what he wanted to say in that moment, or if he was waiting for her to speak. Either way, all he managed was, 'I'll call when I reach the digs,' and jumped out of the car, almost forgetting his rucksack in the back seat.

What he remembers most about that first journey to Limerick is the relief and excitement that filled him the further he travelled. A giddiness grew in him so that it was all he could do not to laugh; his stomach hurt from trying to contain it. A student with greasy hair and a Metallica T-shirt sat next to him at Castleisland but had moved by Newcastle West. He probably thought him mad. That just made him want to laugh more.

He was so happy to get away, but now that memory and those years are loaded with regret and guilt. He left his sisters. He even left his mother, the visitors. Would things be any different now, were he to leave here again?

105

It turns out to be an easy-enough visit. Phil Williams, from Dublin. He is down on holidays with his family for two weeks. There isn't anything particularly wrong with him; he's just been drinking all day and taken a bad turn. He only makes it as far as the wildflowers before tripping over himself and falling on his face. The two of them sit there for a time as Phil's sentences drift in and out of sense. Soon Micheál has convinced him to call his wife, tell her where to pick him up. About twenty minutes later, she appears in a Volvo station wagon. While Micheál speaks to his wife, Claire, letting her know what happened, Phil is already passed out in the passenger seat.

After they leave, he climbs towards the house, his breath threatening to abandon him. He is unsure if Saoirse is still there. He hadn't seen her leave, but then he had been forced to give the visitor most of his attention. He remembers the look on her face when she took in the flashlight, the jumper, and that swell in his chest returns. Feeling nauseous, he opens the front door.

Inside, Saoirse sits on the couch. The food remains in the plates atop the counter, untouched. Micheál sits beside her. Sammy is curled at her feet; he'd stayed with her when the visitor arrived.

'Are you okay?' he asks.

Saoirse stares out the window. 'Áine never really told you anything about the years here after you left, did she? What it was like for us. She told me that ye tended to avoid talking about it.'

'Yeah, but I don't think –'

He falls silent as she turns to look at him. 'I do think. Now shut up and listen.'

CVI

'After you left, Áine took over from you, helping Mam with the visitors. She seemed almost happy about it, at first. You two had such a weird rivalry. Though it became clear soon enough that she didn't care for it at all. Unlike the two of you, I never wanted to do it. I was terrified of being asked, being forced to help. It being my turn. I was, what, fifteen? And I was so angry at Mam for what she was putting the family through, and I was furious at you for leaving. And Áine promised that she wouldn't do what you did; she swore that she'd stay until I finished school. But I guess I was just so unhappy and so scared of being left here alone, with her, with those cliffs, that I couldn't believe her. It got so bad that I was having panic attacks on the school bus home, that I started fucking up my body with a razor, looking for any sort of release. And then, one night, I couldn't take it anymore.

'I waited until an evening when Mam cycled into the village to do a shop, and Áine was in her room, studying. I only knew two things: I didn't want to use the cliffs and I didn't want Mam to be there, because fuck her, and fuck her getting a chance to "save my soul". The bullshit she told herself. So I locked the bathroom door, ran myself a bath, and slit my left wrist. I'd planned to slit both, but I felt faint after the first one and dropped the razor into the water. The worst thing about it, as the blood flowed out of me, was that it still felt like I was falling. Anyway, I must have passed out then because the next thing I remember is waking up in the hospital in Tralee.

'Áine needed to go for a shite – that's what saved me, it seems. She was dying to go and so was banging on the door, demanding I let her in, and when there was no response, she freaked out and broke in the door. I know it's an old door, and light, but still. I keep thinking about how much effort it must have taken to break it down. When she found me, she stopped the bleeding with a towel and rang 999. Apparently, the ambulance passed Mam as she cycled back out the headland with the shopping. I often picture that. The blue swirl of light racing ahead of her, towards the cliffs. What she must have been thinking in those moments.'

107

Out the window, the land is fading into darkness. Micheál watches this unfold, unable now to look in Saoirse's direction. His nausea had worsened as she spoke, a dull ache growing in his shoulder. He must have pulled a muscle when out with the visitor, he thinks, maybe when he lifted the sobbing man upright by the cliff.

'Why did ye never tell me about this?'

'Mam wanted to, but Áine and I convinced her not to, in the end.'

'Why?' he asks, looking at her now.

She shrugs. 'You so clearly wanted out, and we didn't want to drag you back in like that. That was a part of it. But maybe it was also a punishment, something to withhold from you for being such a shit brother. I don't know; it was so long ago now.'

He looks at the exposed portion of her left arm, sees a new motive behind the tattoo.

'Maybe I could have done something, if I'd been there,' he says, trailing off.

Saoirse snorts. 'Don't try and wedge your guilt into my

story, Mick. You aren't the centre of all this, as much as you might like to think that you are. There were more of us involved; we all suffered.'

'I know,' he says.

'Do you, though?' She sighs. 'You know, I've spent most of my life being angry – at her, at you, at this place. I can't do it anymore; I just want to move past it, to feel something other than anger or fear all the time. I want to feel something different.'

'Is that why you came back?'

She nods.

'Saoirse, I'm so sorry for leaving. You know that, right?'

'I know.'

'I think about that, and what I did to Nadine, every day.'

Sammy awakens, looks at both of them, and saunters over to his water bowl. The sound of lapping fills the room.

'You should,' Saoirse says. 'You should carry all your mistakes with you. But, like, you shouldn't make a life-long prison of them, Mick. Instead you should use them, learn from them, to try and be a better fucking person.'

She glances out the window, seeming to realise for the first time how dark it is outside. 'I better get going,' she says.

'You can stay the night if you want?'

She rises from the couch. 'No, no, I don't think I need to do that anymore.' She lifts her jacket off the back of the couch, puts it on. At the door, she turns. 'You know, you talk about how guilty you feel, but there's something you can do to fix all this, and it's something that will help yourself, too. But you won't do it, will you?'

'But what about them?' he says.

'This has never been about them, not really. This has always been about you. It's all on you.'

With that, she leaves.

CVIII

That Sunday afternoon, years ago, when he brought Nadine to the headland for the first time. The look shared between his mother and Áine when he asked where Saoirse was, when they said she was at Stephanie's, studying. He thought nothing of it at the time, too caught up in his own worries. Now he sees a new truth in that look. Sees, once again, his own failings.

109

After Saoirse leaves, Micheál goes straight to the press, takes out the bottle of Jameson. Not as much left as he'd hoped. It was worse than he ever thought, those four years where he deserted his sisters. As often as he reassured himself that nothing happened, that things had been different after he left, he had also imagined many other possibilities, things they suffered through – difficult visitors, winter nights up by the cliffs, their single-minded mother – but he had never envisioned this.

He sits at the kitchen table and drinks the whiskey from

a tea cup, pours himself another. As the alcohol works its way into him, the nausea rises again, the sharp pain in his shoulder radiating upwards towards his neck. He works the shoulder, groans. He must have really done some damage.

His mind returns to what Saoirse told him. If he had stayed, maybe this wouldn't have happened. He could have helped, protected them. No, this was what Saoirse was talking about – bringing everything back to him. Her pain was her story, not his. His guilt was a separate thing. Fuck, though, how brave she was, returning here. Facing up to all that. And how strong Áine had been, breaking down the door, doing her best to shield her from the visits throughout those years. And even remaining in touch with him, treating him as her brother, though for so long he had not lived up to the name. Above the fireplace, Christ throws his eyes to Heaven, the flame where his heart should be long since extinguished.

Micheál finds his gaze drawn to the chair nearest the hallway, his mother's green jumper still cast limply over its wooden frame. Looking at it now, he is reminded of Saoirse's anger the night he offered it to her. And of Helena, her letter, and a thought occurs to him: she likely doesn't know what happened to the heron. In her mind, the bird may well be alive, may even be airborne at this very moment, flying away from this place where it had never belonged.

It is when he tries to stand, and falls back into his chair, that he understands something is wrong. The pain has spread to his jaw now, pulsing. A pressure grows in his back, between his shoulder blades. It feels different than he expected, but he knows what is happening.

He takes his phone from his jeans pocket. Stares at the

lit-up screen. What is the number again? Saoirse mentioned 999, but hasn't it changed? He chances the number. Someone answers. He is transferred to the ambulance services. A woman's voice reaches him. Midlands-sounding, clinical.

He offers her his name, address, informs her, 'I'm having a heart attack.' He is surprised by how matter-of-fact he sounds. As if it is something minor, inconsequential. Or something expected.

'Right, sir; are you alone in the house, sir?'

'I am. Except for Sammy.'

'Could you put him on the phone, so, sir?'

Despite everything, he laughs. 'He wouldn't be much use to you.'

'Sir?'

'He's a dog.'

A pause, then she continues, as if ticking off points on a checklist. 'Okay, sir, if you're alone in the house, I need you to open your front door, so the emergency responders will be able to access your house when they arrive. And I also need you to lock the dog in a room, as it may attack the responders when they appear, particularly if you are unconscious.'

Micheál stands with difficulty. Tired now, his breathing a little strained, he opens the front door. What did she say to do next? He beckons Sammy and starts down the hallway. Opens the door to the visitors' room. 'Go on in there, Sam.' The dog looks at him, an obvious reluctance to his gaze. 'It'll just be for a little bit, I promise. Go on.'

Back in the kitchen, he leans against the counter, the woman asks, 'Do you have any aspirin in the house, sir?'

'I do.'

'Take a dosage, please, sir.'

He struggles to open the press, his strain upwards flaring the pulse in his jaw, his back. Breathing is hard. He palms two tablets into his mouth, sucks water from the tap. He pools on to the chair nearest the front door, hoping the woman won't ask him to do anything else that involves moving. He's unsure if he has the energy to rise again.

The woman continues to speak, though it is a struggle to keep the phone to his ear. He catches the word 'allergies'. A clear pressure on his chest now. An invisible body pressing down.

The woman's voice is suddenly his mother's voice. 'Are there any allergies the responders should be aware of?'

'I need to go.'

'Sir, I need you to stay on the –'

He hangs up, slides the phone into the heart of the table. The immense pressure on his chest, as if the land itself has taken him into it and is pushing him down, down, further down. What Saoirse said before she left. She was right. His refusal to leave is not entirely about the visitors, helping them. *I'm doing this for me.* It is a prison, but it also is a refuge, a place that brings him meaning, purpose.

How has he ended up on the floor? The tile is cold, hard. He thinks he can hear Sammy scratching at the visitors' room door. He looks towards the clock, but it is gone – or at least cut from sight by the hard edge of the kitchen table. Was this the same spot where his mother lay, alone, that night? It had to be close. How had she felt then, if conscious enough to think? Lying here, he accepts that he will never know. The past, for all its texture, rarely talks back.

From where he lies, he can see past the side of the couch and out the window, where Triskmore is a swell of shadow in the moonlight. He sees An Claí Rua, the walkers upon it throughout the centuries, searching out the cliffs. Micheál knows that he has been walking it too, in his own way. Like his parents did before him. What has his life been since Nadine's departure but a longer form of jump and fall? Now that the crash is here, though, he knows, with a sudden, desperate urgency, that this is not what he wants.

And then he is outside, standing among the wildflowers, a huddled jury of stars overhead. He rises towards the cliffs, his breathing suddenly freer, energy returned. As he nears the drop, he acknowledges something he has long known to be true, though not confronted: he never looks down. All these years up at the cliffs, when with a visitor or alone, he avoids glancing down to where sea and land meet.

Maybe this time he will.

When he reaches the cliffs, his gaze drops, and with it he has a sense of falling, as if his body is being pulled downwards, where he now sees waves pounding the cliffs, white foam visible through the darkness.

Looking at waves that seem to almost glow, he thinks how maybe there is a way of resolving all this strife. Threads of an idea have long been in his mind, but he has been reluctant to knit them together. Now, at the edge of his land, he does. He cannot imagine a life for himself away from here. Not completely away. Not yet. But he can make a start.

He will call Áine in the morning, or maybe he will first travel into the village to see Saoirse in person, now that he is feeling better. Yes, it'd be more appropriate to do this in person, to settle things with Saoirse first. He'll come right out with it, tell her he's happy to sell the land, that he's sorry he held out so long. He just has one condition – that once the hotel has been built he is hired in some capacity. A groundskeeper, janitor, he doesn't care. Halloran will go for it, he is certain. The man seems determined to get the land. After talking to Saoirse, he will search out Brenda; maybe he'll even bring her some wildflowers from the field. She'd like that. And he will ask her if, for a little while, just until he gets his act together, he can stay in that attic room. Saoirse will have left by the time all the land-selling business is sorted. And if, like she said, it can fit an orchestra, it will more than do him. Maybe he can even offer to help around the shop. Make himself of some use. This is the first step. He sees it now so clearly. Noise – is it Sammy whining? – reaches him from somewhere nearby, though he can't say where exactly. After that, he should visit Áine. She too deserves an apology in person.

A figure above him. In the sky. No, at the front door. In the house.

A visitor? No, not this time.

Bright light behind the figure, pouring into the house. The feel of cold tile against his hands, cheek. Is it morning already? What is it his mother used to say? When the night passes things will seem different. Hope comes with the morning light.

He thinks that and is calm.

Acknowledgements

My heartfelt thanks to everyone at Granta, especially Laura Barber, for her belief in my work, and for those priceless conversations in the margins that helped elevate the book to another level.

To my agent, Euan Thorneycroft, for his championing of the book, as well as his insightful notes on the manuscript prior to submission. To copyeditor Daphne Tagg and her sharp eye, as well as Jack Smyth, for the stunning cover.

To the Arts Council of Ireland, who generously supported me with an Agility Award and Next Generation Artist Award. I am also grateful to the Arts Council and Kerry County Council for awarding me the position of Kerry County Council Writer in Residence, and to the Munster Literature Centre for supporting me with a Frank O'Connor International Short Story bursary. To Niamh Ní Bhaoill and the team at Sibéal Teo for sending me a copy of their documentary, *Gleann na nGealt*.

To all those who were kind enough to offer feedback on the manuscript at various stages: Claire Kilroy, Cethan Leahy, Tadhg Coakley, Mary Morrissy and Carys Davies. To Billy O'Callaghan and Danielle McLaughlin for the supportive words. I am indebted to Vanessa O'Loughlin for her advice and encouragement. A debt of gratitude is also owed to Sean Lyons, who helped instil a love of literature in me at an early age, and whose guidance has continued over the years. And Victoria Kennefick, whose support, critical eye and, most importantly, friendship was so vital during the writing of this book. Long live Braintrust.

To my family, both the O'Regans and the Murphys. My parents, Denis and Elizabeth, for their unremitting support over the years. I could not have reached this point without you. And to Lisa. Thank you for everything.